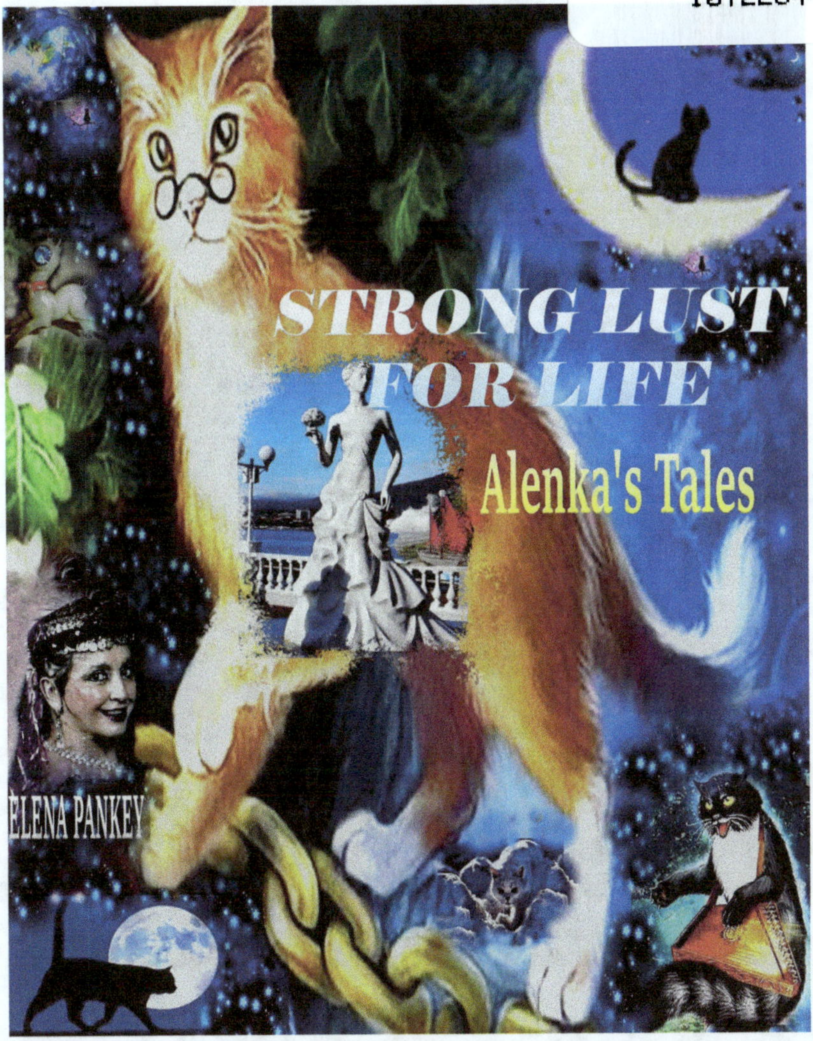

STRONG LUST FOR LIFE

Alenka's Tales

ELENA PANKEY

Strong Lust For Life

Alenka's Tales

Elena Pankey

***

ISBN: 9781952907203

Contents

***

"To everything, there is a season, and a time to every

purpose under the heaven: A time to be born, and a time to die;

a time to plant, and a time to pluck up that which is planted. A

time to kill, and a time to heal; a time to break down and a time

to build up. A time to weep, and a time to laugh; a time to mourn

and a time to dance. A time to cast away stones and a time to gather stones together, a time to embrace, and a time to refrain from embracing. A time to get, and a time to lose; a time to keep, and a time to cast away. A time to rend and a time to sew. A time to keep silence, and a time to speak. A time to love, and a time to hate; a time of war and a time of peace" (Ecclesiastes 3: 1-8).

***

God created the Garden of Eden with many beautiful trees and good fruits. There was the tree of life that can last eternal life, and the tree of knowledge of good and evil that brings death in the middle of the garden (Genesis 2:15-16).

***

Author

The author, Elena Pankey has created many fascinating books in Russian and English, and published them in Europe and America. Among them, it is worth noting several funny books about the lives of cats and dogs, about monuments to beloved animals. Also, her wonderful books about Argentine tango or about the famous Ukrainian artist Valeria Bulat (her 3d ex-husband) cannot be ignored. Moreover, her historical and biographical trilogy about Gelendzhik, memories of her hometown and people who lived there in the 1950-1990s are unusually interesting.

The author has many years of experience in various fields of education, literature, theater, dance, cinematography. She

especially enjoyed the work of a tour guide, traveling with tourists around Russia and the Baltic states. She also shared with people her love of art and knowledge of the museums and palaces of St. Petersburg. After several marriages, she found her true happiness in California.

***

Alenka's Tales

This book has wonderful life stories full of wisdom and fun. It tells about a very curious little girl, who was growing up in the house of her grandparents and loved adventures. There are several fascinating legends about different kind flowers, stubborn lambs, an over proud Rooster, and many other unusual stories collected in this book. It has uniquely done art pieces, complementing stories.

The book has an entertaining story about the rabbits who were sitting under the window, requesting a free supply of carrots; about small songbirds courageously fighting with the crows while protecting their nests; about the young Owl parents who taught their babies how to fly. The book has entertaining and educational stories which are a great tool to overcome fears on the path to success.

***

Fears

Once upon a time, Fear was born on the planet Earth but had nowhere to live. At that ancient time, the Earth was completely empty, and nobody lived on Earth. But soon all sorts of insects and even huge animals began to appear on it. Some of the big beasts were so tall that they reached the sky.

When Fear saw that many different living things came to the Earth, he rejoiced. He immediately flew up to the smallest insect, climbed into it, and settled down there. The insect was not only very small but also it was defenseless and did not know how to resist Fear. And Fear, having settled inside the small bug, soon became dissatisfied with his modest housing. Moreover, he was not having fun inside that submissive insect, which without a fight immediately obeyed Fear, fearing everything around it. That small senseless insect lived poorly while all the time shaking from the Fear. And from the fact that the insect was very afraid of everything, Fear began to grow rapidly inside it and increased in the size. Finally, the little insect was torn by Fear into the small pieces. Then, Fear started looking for a new more spacious housing. Fear walked through the jungle, watching where else to go and settle.

At that far time, a number of different medium-sized and even huge animals walked around in the jungle. There were birds and monkeys in the trees, and even huge Mammoths and Dinosaurs living on the ground. They were grazing peacefully on pastures with densely growing grass.

Once Fear saw the huge animals roaming around, which were much larger than the insect. Fear decided that if he settles inside a huge beast, he himself will grow up and become invincible. So he flew up to the huge Beast, and growled frighteningly, with a terrifying sound, which the Beast had never heard. The Beast was confused. Although he was huge, he did not fight and did not resist Fear, but immediately meekly let Fear into itself.

As soon as Fear settled inside the huge Beast, that Beast became afraid of everything around. And as soon as he started to afraid of everything, he became very weak. The huge Mammoths and Dinosaurs did not resist Fear and soon they all extinct. Fear was gaining strength from everyone who was afraid of him, turned into a huge Monster. He wandered the Earth everywhere found those who were afraid at least of something, and Fear rejoiced, thinking that he was invincible.

***

Many millennia have passed, and finally, Man appeared on the Earth. People were different and some of them had a small

and submissive Soul. Fear very quickly got inside such small souls and began his reign in the weak people. The Souls of such weak people were quickly put up with the difficult conditions of their lives. Fear grew inside them, killing a submissive, all fearing Soul. People without Souls supporting them could not continue to live and quickly died.

But some People had shining eyes and courageous hearts. Their Soul also was fearless and such real People were afraid of almost nothing. When Fear was coming close to them, they pushed it back, preventing it from entering their Souls. Courageous People kept their beautiful Soul in a pristine, solid vessel and protected it. When Fear met the resistance of such courageous people, it faded and became less and less powerful. And fearless People became stronger and stronger. But Fear remained nearby, watching everything around and waiting for the moment to inhabit a fearing person.

***

Magical Gelendzik

There are not many good things are getting done fast. And the fairy tales don't add up quickly. Once upon a time, in the faraway kingdom under the name Russia, there was a small health resort named Gelendzik. The gorgeous town Gelendzik was located on the coast of the Black Sea. It was lying down at the foot of the high Caucasus mountain ridges and settling on the coast of the Black Sea. This beautiful town was drowning in gardens and hid in the bright greenery and flowers.

There were the vineyards surrounding it, and it was looking like a green border of lace. Blue waves were splashing on the coastal sand. The seagulls were circling above the waves, looking for some fish. The people were rightly proud that the town was so beautiful. However, it was so small that nobody could even find it on the map. But people heard about some magnificent fairy tales that lived in each corner of that enchanted town.

Once upon a time a very strict Minai and his kind wife Anna lived in the beautiful Gelendzik. And they were raising their little granddaughter Alenushka. Also, they had a very wise cat Murka, who was a Fairy.

Alenushka had a beautiful, golden-haired mother with a German name – Emma—given by her father Minai. Young Emma was very trustful and dreamed of happiness. One day a seductive demon, Konstantin, bewitched her. He became

Alenushkas' father, but rarely visited the young mother and the baby. After that, the joy of life flew away from Emma, and her gray-blue eyes most all the time were sad.

All mothers' troubles and concerns are reflected in a child. So, one day mother Emma brought Alenushka to a doctor. A little girl saw that her mother was afraid of the injection. The mother's Fear immediately

flew over to the child and settled inside the girl.

One stormy day of autumn 1956, a big flood began in Gelendzik. Konstantin could not come fast enough to help Emma and the baby to escape the distress. The young Emma was afraid of the flood quickly rising on the floor of her poor, small hut.

Also, she could not cope alone with this huge Fear. Fear always brings frustration and anger to people. Seeing her miseries, Fear started to grow bigger and bigger, ruling in Emma, making her threaten and curse at everyone around.

When Alenushka' father finally came to them, he could not stand hearing Emma's anger and blames. Konstantin also felt Fear and did not want to fight it. This merciless Fear made him leave the hut and his helpless family, and he went far away. His biggest Fear was the Fear of Failure, as in many other people. He did not know that any person who surrenders under the pressure of Fear would not live a long or happy life? because Fear eats people's Souls.

When this flood covered the floor of Emma's little house, she took Alenushka in her arms and ran to her parent's house. However, Emma did not find any comfort in the house of her stern father Minai. When Alenushka was only one year old, Emma went far away to work in the distant land in the thirtieth kingdom. This kingdom was in the East, on the island of Sakhalin in the Pacific Ocean, where Emma was making some money for the future dream house. For seven years little Alenushka has been raised by the love and care of her grandmother Anna, kind Fairy.

***

Grandparents

Alenushka's' grandparents lived in a small, dark, and poor cabin with three rooms. One "summer room" was always very cold and served as a repository for vegetables, fruits, pickles, and jams, which grandmother made and collected during summer. The main room with a huge stove was a kitchen. The stove was tall under the ceiling and it always smoked when grandmother cooked something, like porridge or potato. Later, there will be a special story about that magical stove, where Alenushka spent many hours escaping the freezing winter. Little Alenushka slept with her grandmother in the kitchen on the old metal bed. That room had also a small table where grandmother served some modest food. The laundry grandmother did by hands and outside of the house using a special wooden board with metal ribs on it. Then she ironed clean clothes by an old cast iron, which was heated on the stove.

The third and warmest room belonged to grandfather

and served him as an office and bedroom. Alenushka was not allowed to go there. But sometimes Alenushka was looking into the crack of his door. She saw him sitting there at a huge table reading numerous newspapers. He subscribed to the newspapers by mail, and bound them into the huge bundles, collecting by the date.

In his room grandfather Minai had a huge desk with a green fabric top. That special table had a lot of secret lockers on the sides of it, and grandfather kept them all locked. But sometimes he would forget to lock his desk when he would go to his secret room behind the house. He had a wonderful hobby - photography, and was spending many hours developing and printing his photos.

It seemed that grandfather Minai knew no love or care for anyone in the house. He was not a faithful or loving husband, and grandmother often complained that he had a terrible character. He was very strict with his granddaughter and often punished Alenushka for all her various pranks. So, by following the Russian fairy tale, Alenushka called her grandfather "Gorenych." .

Alenushka was growing up as a curious and a little bit

mischievous child. She loved to ask a lot of questions, but adults shrugged her off like from an annoying fly. However, among themselves they often whispered about something important, which concerned her fate. Alenushka did not like to feel that she lived among so many secrets and wanted to solve them by all means. Therefore, she looked everywhere to find out about the secrets that were hidden from her.

Most of all, Alenushka valued adventures and could not help herself, but looked in all prohibited places. One day when her grandfather was absent, she made her way into his room. Despite the ban, she tried to open the little doors of his magic table and see what was inside the lockers.

Despite the punishments threatening her, Alenushka still had a lot of curiosity about everything. The girl continued to poke her nose everywhere. Sometimes she accidentally would break something, or take something without permission. After doing something that she was not supposed to do, the little girl tried to run away from her grandfather's punishments to the garden or hide under the bed. But grandfather would find her and put her in a corner on her knees, demanding an apology, and her promises of "never to act badly again." It was even worse when he put some sharp seeds or peas on the floor and forced Alenushka to stand on it by her bare knees. The peas dug into the girl's bare knees, leaving deep red dents. But Alenushka was a very proud and stubborn girl. She did not want to humiliate herself by begging forgiveness from the person she did not respect. Also, more often than not, she considered herself innocent. Although standing in the dark corner of the cold room was unpleasant, especially on the sharp peas, she endured, despite the hellish pain. However, it did not stop her from doing something prohibited in the future. Her curiosity was stronger than any punishment.

Alenushka did not have many friends. Her best friend was Natasha Ponasenko, who lived near the Meadow, and they often played together. One day she came to visit Alenushka. Most often they played hide and seek or catch-up. So one day Natasha chased after Alenushka. But there was nowhere to run, except for the open door of the house, and Alenushka ran there with all her speed.

The day before, Grandmother had gathered a lot of chicken eggs and laid them in a corner on the cold floor for safety. There were no windows in the room. After the bright sunlight, it was impossible to make out what was laying down on the floor. After a bright sunny day, the room was very dark. In addition, Alenushka was running with all her might, escaping from her friend, and could not stop. By the inertia, she ran through the whole pile of eggs that her grandmother kept there. Then, in addition, she slipped on them and fell into the very middle of the yellow mess.

Then, such a cry arose! The frightened friend Natasha was immediately sent home, and forbidden to come to Alenushka in the future. Then, Grandfather chased after his granddaughter, holding a huge stick in his hands. And he swung it at the little girl. But his wife Anna always defended a not obedient granddaughter or hid her from grandfather's heavy stick or strong belt.

So was it this time. Grandmother covered the girl by her body from the punishment by the cruel grandfather Gorenych. The heavy stick fell on her. And immediately her hands became dark-blue from the hit. She cried out: "*You could have killed the child, monster*!" And she led the crying granddaughter run into the garden.

Cat Murka followed them. This tender cat always rubbed against the girl's legs, showing her love and comforting Alenushka. In the garden, Alenushka had many friends who loved her: rabbits, bees, birds, dogs, and ants. When she would go to the garden, her cat and devoted dogs would follow her there. They looked with love into her eyes trying to console her. Grandmother stroked Alenushka on her head and whispered: "My poor orphan. We will write to your mother about the atrocities of the grandfather. Maybe she will come soon, visit and protect you."

Alenushka thought that her caring grandmother was a kind Fairy. In reality, her grandmother was a storyteller and a folk healer. She often treated her granddaughter by useful herbs, and taught her how to use them. Moreover, grandmother was teaching the little girl some life wisdom and how to live in harmony with nature. But the girl often dismissed all this teaching, and loved to do everything in her own way.

Most importantly, Grandmother was a very kind and caring woman. A long time ago, her two sons had flown from the native nest to Moscow. Maybe this is why Grandmother Anna loved her first granddaughter Alenushka very much and spent her little free time with her. In the evenings, she combed the long Alenushka braids and pronounced: "The braid is girlish beauty." Before going to bed, she told Alenushka the old fairy tales or sang Russian songs. Grandmother knew many wonderful songs, and she taught her granddaughter to sing them. Every night before going to bed, Good Fairy Anna told Alenushka different tales. One summer night she told a very frightening story about the ever lived Fear. Many grandmothers' tales will come later in this book.

***

Black Sea

A delightful paper reproduction of sea painting was hanging in grandfather's room. That painting was done by well-known artist of 19th century, Ivan Aivazovsky, and was called "The Capture of a Turkish Boat by Russian Sailors and the Release of Captured Caucasian Women, 1880".

Sometimes, when grandfather was not at home, Alenushka loved to come to the grandfather room, climbed on the bed and admired the painting. She enjoyed staying there for a long time dreaming about being in a wonderful fairy tale.

One day, after a good dinner, when her grandmother was washing dishes, she got courage, went to her grandfather and asked him: *"Why our city is called Gelendzhik?"*

Grandfather Minai reluctantly put down his newspaper. But he wanted to show off his knowledge, and so he began to say: "Once upon a time, Greek immigrants from Turkey established a colony here and named it Torik. In the XV century, the city became part of the Ottoman Empire. It was the place of export of young slaves to Turkish harems. "Gelendzhik" in Turkish means "white bride". But at that moment, the grandmother interrupted him, saying that it was time for the girl to sleep, and not to listen about "slaves and harems".

Indeed, the girls' eyes stuck together either from the smoked kerosene lamp or from the fatigue. Grandfather immediately looked very angry and did not talk this evening at all. Alenushka sadly went to the stove and climbed on the top of it. There her cat Murka was already waiting for her, comfortably curled into a ball. Cat Murka said: "Today the moon is full. At night we will go to the garden. I'll tell you more interesting tales there and show some miracles. In the meantime, get some sleep."

The grandmother worked from dawn to dusk in the house: cooked, washed, ironed, and took care for her husband and her granddaughter. But in the morning with the sunrise she ran to the garden to do exercises and work. Then, she ran to the sea to swim. The sea was five blocks from the house and was called "Black." Alenushka loved to ask a lot of questions. So, having heard that they have the "Black Sea," she did not believe it. Sometimes, she was taken to the sea and saw that the sea was transparent and sometimes greenish-blue.

Alenushka had long noticed that the main thing for all adults was to make children listen to them attentively. After that, they became kinder and were ready to do more than any child expected. Most of the time, Alenushka tried to stay away from her grandfather. But when her grandfather was in a good mood, he could tell something interesting. So, from time to time, Alenushka would approach him and ask about the name of the city or about the Black Sea. In a good mood her grandfather liked to talk. Once after dinner, Alenushka found a good moment when her grandfather was happy and asked him different questions.

Then, she listened to him without interruption and learned an incredible story. Her grandfather Minai said: "There are many nationalities of people living in Gelendzik. Every nation has its own version of how the name to the sea was given. In the time of Ancient Russia, the Black Sea was called Russian, because Russian Prince of Kiev visited its shores. The Italians, who owned small ports in the middle Ages, called the Sea of Pontus. The Scythians called it Dark Sea.

For many centuries, the Turks conquered the shores of the Black Sea, and found the fierce resistance of the local tribes, the Circassians and others. Therefore, they called it "Inhospitable Sea". One of the Turkish legends says that in the Black Sea lies the sword of God, which was cast into the sea by a wizard named Ali. The waters of the sea do not want this sword, trying to throw it out of their bowels. When the sea is worried it becomes dark, and even black.

But most likely it has more natural explanation. There is a lot of hydrogen sulfide in the depths of the Black Sea, which corrodes metal objects to a black color. Ancient sailors saw their anchors become black and began to call it - Black Sea. Even before our era, the first settlements of the Greeks appeared on the shores of the Black Sea."

Every time somebody would say word "Greeks" Alenushka would be alert. It was not customary at all to talk about Greeks in the family. Much later, the girl learned the tragedy of her beautiful mother Emma, who fell in love with a handsome Greek, the young man Konstantin. In the horrible Stalin terror of 1938, Konstantin's father (as many other local Greeks) was shot down without a trial. He was called an "enemy of the people" only because he had vineyards, and some poor people worked for him collecting grapes and doing the wine.

A retired major, Minai forbade his daughter Emma from dating the "evil demon" Konstantin. Emma's heart was broken, and she was not able to find her happiness in Gelendzhik. So, she left her little daughter to be raised by her mother Anna, and went to work on the far Sakhalin Island.

"Well, what can I say about Sakhalin? The weather is beautiful on the island," – the grandmother once sang to Alenushka when the girl asked about her mother. Grandmother had a strong and beautiful voice. She enjoyed singing to her

granddaughter and taught her many Russian songs. It was an education for Alenushka, as well.

***

Summer

Summer was the most favorite time for Alenushka. All surrounding was filled with the sound of cicadas. This sound was reaching its zenith to the highest intensity and happiness of life at noon. Many relatives from all over the Soviet Union gathered at the house from May to October. During that time grandmother's sons visited her from Moscow. Then Alenushka got some protection from the strictness of her grandfather. But most importantly, the uncles played with her. They took her on their shoulders, swing her, or threw her up so high that she was breathless. And even more joyful was the fact that they always brought some presents or surprises for her. It was a real celebration because no one else gave gifts to the girl.

The guests always took the girl to the beach to enjoy the sea and sand. They went down to the sea near the port, where the cafe "Lakomka" was. At that time the beach was rocky, and everywhere strongly smelled of algae, where strange small marine life swarmed in the beach mud.

The sea was the most amazing creature in the summer life. Every day, like an exquisite coquette who did not want to lose her lover, the sea changed its appearance. And nobody could guess how it will look tomorrow. The sea was always new, and it was impossible to stop loving the sea. In summer, the sea most often looked like a gentle, meek, wild animal tamed for a while. The surf quietly and monotonously splashed at the very feet, filling the soul with peace and serenity. You could admire water forever, forgetting everything in the world.

Sometimes Alenushka tried to remember what she saw for the very first time in her life. It was a moment when she swam with some small fish in a huge wheel from a truck. Alenushka looked under the water and enjoyed the wonderful multi-colored bottom of the sea inside the tire. But the most interesting thing was to look into the eyes of the fish and ask if they were worried about her presence there. The fish was always silent. And Alenushka thought that the fish is not as intelligent as her dogs, who talked to her a lot in the garden.

When they were sitting on the rocky beach Alenushka

loved to look at the bay, where sailboats and fishing ships showed off. And other times she was happy just wandering around the beach, looking under her feet and admiring the silvery round stones under the water. But she did not collect sea stones, as before. When they dried, they no longer shone but were "like a woman washing off cosmetics" (according to my grandmother's expression). Sometimes, if she was lucky, Alenushka would find on the shore a large black tire from a car and lie in it. She thought about all kinds of miracles of the world and "vicissitudes of fate," as her grandmother would say. The sun gilded her skin to the darkest shade of pine resin. And round, rustling waves splashed nearby, caressing and calming her soul. The water was very clear and warm. Someone said that she was like "fresh milk".

Alenushka early learned how to swim and dive. After swimming in the sea, her skin became soft and clean, and all abrasions and wounds quickly healed. Once she asked a friend to let her rest on the water mattress. She closed her eyes and the waves slowly carried her away from the beach. It was like another Fairy tale by itself. Another time, Alenushka saw the black anchors on the pier, which were lifted with the sea mud.

Then, she understood why the sea had name "Black". The sea also reminded her of Pushkin's fairy tale "The Golden Fish".

The little girl trusted adults, asked many questions, and often took their answers as the facts. From time to time, she pretended to play, wandering nearby, trying to listen to what adults were whispering about. One of her relatives said that the endless questions were annoying for everyone, and that a child should not get stuck in the adult conversations. However, Alenushka considered her questions very smart and correct. She wanted to know something important about her life, some secret that they discussed and hid from her.

The most important for a child was that she always felt that her grandmother defended her everywhere, even in the distance. She felt that her grandmother was sending her magical energy and the power of her great love. And later anywhere in the world, wherever Alenushka lived, she always felt her grandmother's invisible protection.

***

Dreamlike Garden

In the grandmother's garden, Alenushka often saw a bright

light shining down on her and shimmering in different colors. It was giving her some warmth, joy, and a confident feeling of future happiness. Many trees and flowers brought an absolutely unbelievable fragrance to the garden. That incredible aroma has always been remarkably easy and calming to the girl.

Alenushka spent most of Summer time in the magical garden behind the house. In this enchanted land of flowers and fruits, insects, and various small living creatures, one could remain for many hours, hiding from all problems and troubles. The aromatic plants gave her all the joy of life, and she felt very secure there. Even when a black and fast viper snake suddenly appeared, everyone froze for a moment, and then life rejoiced again.

It was in the dreamlike garden of her grandmother Anna, the good Fairy. Alenushka watched living beings in the garden, and learned to understand their language, their thirst for life. Alenushka learned that many wonderful creatures carefully and cheerfully lived together there. They all were her friends and were teaching her how to achieve all the most important things in life, how to overcome all obstacles on the road to a dream.

One day there Alenushka saw a bright, magical stream of light flowing from above and calming her feelings. The Living Soul of the Garden loved, caressed, and protected the girl. There, in the overgrown garden, sitting under the fragrant bushes and among the flowers, the little girl dreamed of her future wonderful life. Then she would come out of the garden with a sense of relief and renewal, full of new strength, with a new desire to live and love everything around.

Since her childhood, the free-growing, cheerful power of the garden has been the most influential teacher for the girl. At least she felt that the garden Spirit loved her, like nobody else. The spirit of the garden always gave her comfort and joy. Slowly, her soul was the soul of that beautiful garden where she grew up. The wisdom of nature created her character and shaped the soul of the girl.

***

Love for Freedom

The garden was teaching many great lessons. It was providing food and shelter for wildlife, for all birds and insects. While sitting there in the bushes Alenushka trusted all around her. She listened to the bewitching sounds of nature, watched the birds singing in the trees, and the "ladybug," which suddenly would fly to the girl and trustingly sit in her palm.

Alenushka was curious about everything. She loved to lie on the grass and look at the ant's hard work. They were always in a hurry, always busy with something useful. They were building their underground dwellings and stocking up provisions for the winter. Sometimes one ant was dragging a huge wand on itself, which was twice bigger than him. Often his friends ran up to him and helped him with such a huge but important baggage. Sometimes, Alenushka put some bread crumbs in front of the ant or made other obstacles in its way. Then, she admired how the ants were helping each other to overcome the problems. Theses ants taught Alenushka about hard work and friendship.

There were many fragrant flowers in the garden and the bees loved them. One day Grandmother collected apricots in the garden. And the girl and her cat Murka were sitting in flowers and watched the working bees. Alenushka loved to watch the bees. Many honey bees often flew into the garden to collect the healing honey. First, they would find sweet flowers, get inside them, and collected the pollen around their legs. Then they fly back to their hive, and put that honey pollen in their honeycombs. In winter, they feed their honey to their Queen Bee.

The Queen of the Bees was huge and voracious. So, the bees worked from sunrise to sunset only with one goal: to feed the Bee Queen. Alenushka loved to watch the soothing buzz of bees, and always was surprised at their hard work. They had no time to be distracted by any fuss, there was no need to fight or attack someone. Suddenly, one careless, young and trustful bee sat down on Alenushka hand. The girl wanted to take the bee to show it her grandmother. But her cat Murka immediately said:

"Do not be afraid, the bee will not sting if you do not touch it. The bee will rest and fly away. But if the bee feels danger, it will fight for its freedom. Her sting is her only weapon. At the same time, in her sting she keeps her life. Therefore, bees rarely bite. The bee knows that she will die if she gives her sting away. But sometimes, some fearless bees are sure that their freedom is more precious than her life in captivity".

But the girl did not listen to the wise cat. In addition, the Fear already got inside her and whispered: *"Push away the*

On the other hand, the bee tried to protect herself, stung the girl's finger. Alenushka regretted that she did not listen to her wise cat Murka, and felt sorry about the hardworking bee that lost her life because of the girl's curiosity. For a long time Alenushka remembered this lesson of a fearless bee, and she thought that if someone would attack her, she must fight to the end.

Also, the girl remembers that her grandmother told her: *"Transform any fear into action, and it will disappear. Never let fear decide your future."* So, every time when Fear crept up to her, hissing all sorts of horrors, Alenushka told herself that she was stronger than Fear.

***

In the spring, everything was cheerfully and joyfully chirping and ringing. After many showers of rain, the land enjoyed the sunshine, and was getting warm like it was breathing. There were many apricot, cherry, and apple trees in the garden, which all bloomed almost simultaneously. White fluffy branches of cherries were stretching towards the sun. Apricot and apple blossoms attracted the May beetles. Alenushka felt that she could hear the grass and flowers waking, pushing out from the under the dirt moving up. The yellow and white daffodils bloomed near the houses. Some flowers were changing color, and all fruit trees were calling honey bees to pollinate them. The incredibly pleasant and fragrant smell of the spring was flying around the whole house.

The garden fed the family for all summer and autumn. Every year the trees and bushes generously gave a lot of fresh, varied, fragrant, and delicious food. There were many bushes of beloved black and red currants, black and white grapes in the garden. The prickly bushes of the favorite blackberries with juicy berries were signaling and beckoning from the ditch. She especially loved to crawl under a grape bush and pick up directly by her lips the small, black, and very sweet grapes. Whatever she could find there in the garden was her main food source for the whole day. Also, the garden never knew any chemicals and had healthy plants. So, Alenushka could eat anything right there from the trees and bushes.

Every spring, grandmother planted various vegetables. Often she asked her husband Minai to go to the garden to spray the trees or vegetables to help her to control the pests. The lower part of the trees he smeared with lime to protect them from the various insects. But the grandfather did not like to work in the garden. But grandmother tried to stock up a big amount of potatoes for the winter. When her grandmother worked in the garden, she would say: *"What you sow, you will reap."*

After much persuading, Minai slowly walked there with a shovel to dig the fresh potatoes. Alenushka job was to walk behind him and collect the pink potatoes in the basket. And grandmother pooled all weeds around them. Then, she cooked the potato with the peel ("jacket potato"), and fresh potatoes with fresh tomato were incredibly tasty. There was very little rain in the summer, and plants were fighting for survival. The garden was refreshingly casual, connecting with the natural landscape. However, all vegetables needed to be watered. In the courtyard was a deep well with always very cold, crystal-clear drinking water. But the well was very far from the garden, and the grandmother did not have watering hoses. In the summer in the heat, all irrigation should be done by hand.

Grandmother carried water from the well to the garden in

a bucket or in a large watering can. Alenushka also had a small watering can. That entire job was unusually tiring, long, and hard. They had to go back and forth, pulling the water from the well, and carrying it in the heavy watering can back to the rows of vegetables. The water in the watering can quickly was ending and Alenushkas' disappointment was huge because she did not water even in the half of the vegetables.

Once in childhood, the grandmother, Good Fairy Anna, was teaching Alenushka the basic law of gardening and life: *"It is to grow in ourselves, to develop the seeds of kindness, honesty and compassion. This is what you will collect later. Remember that your garden and your soul are a microcosm of the world. Plan and create a new look for it. So that when you walk with various zigzags and turns along your garden path, to discover surprise or admiration at every step."*

Then, she continued: *"Try to be kind, honest and compassionate. That's what you will harvest. Then, share the blessings and abundance of your garden, whether it is in the form of fruits, flowers, herbs or vegetables".* However, over time, without the water and care of the kind grandmother, the garden began to perish. In the end, it finally became desolate, merged with the dry landscape, and then finally withered. This is what happens to everything without care and love.

***

Stop Being Afraid

In the childhood mother Emma could not protect Alenushka from different Fears. And Fear began to grow inside Alenushka. Fear lived inside her and often tormented the girl for various reasons, preventing her from sleeping. Alenushka did not know how to deal with Fear. And over time, many different Fears spun around her. Therefore, her life seemed unbearable. But once a wise Fairy, loving Grandmother Anna, said to her granddaughter,

"Do not be afraid of Fear. Fear is strong only as long as you are afraid of something. When you stop being afraid, Fear will run away from you".

Alenushka was very surprised at such a simple solution. She had long wanted to defeat Fear. One night, Alenushka decided to start fighting Fear. She got up and went for a walk in the dark garden. Fear immediately woke up, too, and walked alongside the girl, while whispering all sorts of different small fears into her Soul.

However, loving Cat Murka ran nearby. Cat Murka loved to walk everywhere. She loved her freedom, was independent and was not afraid of anything. Long ago, in her feline childhood, the Cat Murka did not live in Grandma's house. When she was a small kitten, she lived in the wild in the Terrible Forest. There, in order to survive, Murka kitten learned to overcome Fear and catch mice for food.

When Cat Murka was taken into the house, she immediately started to care for Alenushka. The cat slept with her on the top of the old fashioned stove and comforted her in various troubles. Cat Murka often told Alenushka different and wise tales. Also, she always accompanied the girl wherever she went, guarding her from all sorts of misfortunes and protecting her from Fear. Sometimes Cat Murka told her: *"If you feel that Fear is creeping closer and closer to you, tell yourself that you are not afraid of it. Repeat this until the Fear would run away."*

During some nights, when Alenushka wanted to go to the dark garden, Cat Murka ran next to Alenushka and encouraged her, repeating:

"Do not be afraid of anything! I am next to you. I'll bite everyone who has intention to hurt you. I will protect you!!"

Alenushka and her Cat Murka went for a walk around the garden, and did not find anything terrible there. Then, they returned home and went to sleep again. At that night, the girl's Soul was resting and rejoicing grew up and became stronger.

***

One Moon For All

In childhood, Alenushka had one strange, peculiar characteristic. When the full moon brightly illuminated all the paths of the garden, she got out of bed and, without waking up, walked to the garden with her eyes closed.

People apprehensively called Alenushka a "sleepwalker," and less kind people called her as a "lunatic". But these night walks gave her a lot of comforting energy. And later, in her youth, this kind of passionate inner force that was produced by the night wanderings under the moon turned into an incredibly strong and alluring force. Sometimes Alenushka used it playfully to conquer all who met her on the way.

But as a child, Alenushka was very happy while traveling

in the sleep without waking up. Sometimes her kind Fairy, Grandmother Anna, carefully followed the granddaughter, trying to protect her from all sorts of misfortunes. Of course, the old, wise cat Murka always accompanied the girl, as if guarding her.

When Alenushka was already sitting in the garden, the cat would also sit down nearby. Cat Murka was purring while rubbing on the girl's body and comforting her. Alenushka missed her mother Emma.

The loving cat Murka was a mother herself many times. She knew that type of longing for the lost loved children, dear creatures that disappeared forever.

Gorenych took her kittens in the unknown direction. She never saw them again and missed them. Loving Murka tried to comfort the girl:

- *"We all belong to One Moon. This moon shines for all birds and animals, for all-all people on the Earth. We need to love our one Moon and live in*

peace."

Cats do not purr with each other, but they always purr with humans. Cats believe that their purr is that perfect language that a person also speaks. So they hum to people all their desires. Some people understand their cats, as Alenushka understood Murka.

Once, at night, a frightened grandmother found her granddaughter on the garden grass. Alenushka was talking to the moon. The grandmother knew that it was very dangerous to wake up children "walking in a dream". So, she was just whispering her name very quietly. Alenushka woke up, looked around, and then forgot all the wisdom that the Moon and the cat Murka were telling her about. Grandmother took the girl to the dark, cold house.

But cat Murka ran nearby and then, sat next to the bed and started to reassure the girl in her love and whispered to her:

Don't worry, Alenushka. I'll bring you back to the magic garden. And the fabulous Moon will help us to learn many new secrets. But now remember one of our fun fairy tales: "A furry cat is wandering around the garden. A horned goat walks after the cat. Meow-meow ". And Alenushka sweetly fell asleep again, sharing with her grandmother the only one bed of the house.

***

Rooster

One large family of chickens lived in the grandmother Anna courtyard. The chicken house was in the barn, where under the poor, full of holes roof, the grandfather built several shelves for the hens. The grandmother put some hay there for the hens' comfort. The hens laid eggs there, dreaming of raising new chicks.

During the day, the hens walked everywhere and collected everything edible from the ground, usually all kinds of plant seeds. In the evening, grandmother went out into the yard with a bag of different grains. She called for the chickens (cip-cip-cip), and threw them the seeds of wheat or corn. The hens rushed to her and screamed: *"Oh, faster, faster! The sun is going down! We must have time to eat more, and then to run to our shelter to lay eggs."*

In the yard only one Rooster lived among the hens. He was huge, strong and beautiful. He was the Master of the House.

The Rooster was sure that Alexander Pushkin had written a fairy tale about him under the name "The Cock-The Golden Scallop." Alenushka was very fond of Pushkin's fairy tales, and knew many of them by the heart.

Grandmother gave Rooster the name "Peter", and in the evening she was calling him: *"Peter-Peter! Go eat!"* At

sunset the grandmother poured some grain for all hens. But the Rooster was the first to have the dinner. No one dared to eat a grain near him. The Rooster fluttered his colorful wings, and was not in a hurry to come to her. When he was already full, then the hens could also try something. The grandmother said that the Rooster has a tendency to "narcissism". He looked and acted as any narcissistic person would act. Alenushka later asked her about who was that Narcisse. But the story about it will come later.

The Rooster kept the distance with everyone, and everybody understood his importance, respected the Rooster, and the hens went away, giving him more space. The Rooster felt that he was a very special, important and a handsome bird. He tyrannically established his own order in the yard. And all the hens followed his rules, not daring to disobey him. He required all chickens to call him by name and patronymic "Rooster-Petukhovich". Many other living creatures, including Alenushka, were slightly afraid of the wrath of the cocky Rooster-Petukhovich. This huge Rooster was a pretty serious person. He could run after the girl and painfully pinch her if she was in his way to sovereignty.

He loved walking around the courtyard with an important look, and listening to grandmother's song: - *"Cockerel, cockerel, Golden Scallop, silk and buttery head. Why do you get up early and sing so loudly? Let Alenushka sleep more."*

Rooster loved attention, and after this song, he became a little friendlier, and allowed to be stroked gently. Rooster-Petukhovich had many reasons to feel important. He was proud that he worked as an alarm clock. He got up in the morning before everyone else and crowed loudly when it was still dark outside: -*"Good morning! What a lovely day comes!"*

Then Grandmother got up to start the stove and to cook something while scolding Gorenych for his idleness. Alenushka woke up from the smoke of the stove and ran to the garden to greet the yard animals. Also, Rooster-Petukhovich was proud that his hens laid brown eggs. These eggs were not golden and still they were very valuable. The orange-red chickens like their father hatched from the brown eggs. Rooster-Petukhovich has already risen more than one generation of chickens. But most of them went to the chicken soup for Gorenych. When Alenushka was sick, her grandmother cooked for her the chicken soup, as well, saying that it helps recovering quickly.

Rooster-Petukhovich was especially proud of this fact that he serves for the benefit of mankind (by sending his chicks to become a healing soup).

But he also dreamed big, and once tried to fly over the fence. However, grandfather Minai saw it and slightly cut the tips of the Rooster's wings so that he would not dream of flying away. But the Rooster still waved his wings, and crowed loudly while announcing: - *"I am the most beautiful and strong Rooster on the Earth. I can do anything I want."*

Grandfather-Gorenych sarcastically smiled and said: *"One day you might be just a lovely chicken soup, if you would not be so selfish"*.

Rooster also was a very jealous type. In the kingdom of the hens, there was no place for another Rooster. When the new chicken-boys grew up, they were fighting with each other over the ownership of the hens and competed with the main Rooster. But the main Rooster wanted to be the only King. He did not want to have any competition. Therefore, most of the new chicken-boys often were sent to the soup.

Once, when Alenushka was very sick, it was time to cook chicken soup. Gorenych closed the Rooster and all hens in the chicken coop, except for one. Then he called Grandmother Anna that she would bring her granddaughter to the yard. When Alenushka came out of the house, she saw a huge stump by the ditch and Gorenych had a huge, sharp ax in his hand. He took the chicken by her legs, put it on a stump and chopped off her head. A commotion and a cry started in the chicken coop. The hen with its detached head still ran around the yard for some time and waved its wings.

The grandfather said, with an evil hint: - *"Here is the headless chicken running around, like a stupid woman."*

Grandmother thought that it was a hint on his daughter Emma. She got upset, and went to the house getting ready to make a lunch. That episode was a big shock for Alenushka, as well. Moreover, she was hungry and ran back to the house, looking for some food. But there was nothing to eat there. In a minute, that headless chicken fell down motionless. Then, grandmother took the chicken, put a frying pan under her neck, and collected the dripping blood. She fried chicken blood and gave it to eat to the girl, saying that now her granddaughter will recover from her anguish yearning quickly. The hungry girl did not know what she was eating. She was still worrying about the headless chicken running around and her grandfather's hints about it. She did not want to be such a stupid chicken in their town.

* * *

Generosity

When a fence was built around the grandmother's house, a big rabbit's family made a home under the large bushes. The yard dogs did not want to hunt rabbits or run after squirrels very often. But still rabbits were afraid of everything and did not go far from their bushes. They were hiding there from the dogs and all other danger of the garden, feeling happy and well protected. Sometimes Alenushka saw they would come out to be on the sun and enjoy the beautiful day. One of them began to suntan on the rocks, periodically turning over and stretching his legs.

Their big Father rabbit lived a little bit further, outside of the fence. But every day at dinnertime he visited his ever-present family to spend the evenings or weekends and holidays. They all usually had their dinner around the time of sunset.

Mother-rabbit and her big family have eaten all the weeds nearby. All around her was already just bare ground. Mother rabbit and her always growing family have been eating all they could find nearby without going to the dangerous far end of the garden. Near their rabbit house was growing only green but poisonous bushes of the narcissus. Even though the rabbits were very hangry, they knew what was good for their health, and what was bad. The long, juicy leaves of the narcissus looked so green and delicious, but the rabbits could not eat them.

One day Alenushka saw under the window that Mother rabbit was eating rose petals.   First, she smelled the beautiful fragrance of the rose, and knew that it was edible.   Then, she stood up on her back legs and stretched a little up to get to the flower. Sometime, they all were sitting under the window and looking up, clearly saying: - *"Alenushka! Go to the garden and bring us some delicious green grass. There is so much of it in the garden"*.

Alenushka listened to them, saw their smart faces, and wanted to help them. She went to the garden, collected some fresh grass and put it near the rabbits bush. They were delighted with new green food that fell from the sky, as they thought.

One day grandmother bought a huge bag of carrots. Alenushka wanted to feed rabbits, thinking that the bag would last for several months. Every day she threw several huge carrots to the garden. However, all carrots very quickly were gone completely. Soon the huge bag that grandmother wanted to have for the winter was also empty. Rabbits happily looked up, saying: - *"Oh! This heaven sent us precious food as a gift! Thank you, God, for your generosity and for that rain of abundance! We hope your kindness would never end, and we would not need to work anymore for the food."*

Near the house of the rabbit, a squirrel with a big fluffy tail happily lived, as well. She often came out to chew something in the garden, as well. Especially, squirrel loved the oranges from the orange tree which grew nearby. Also, they were very good climbers and climbed up to the apricot or almond trees, and ate all the fruits that still were on the branches. Alenushka asked her grandfather to wrap the tree trunks with metal sheets, and squirrels would not clime up to eat delicious fruits.

***

Flowers

Outside of the fence, and not far from the house, there was a magical meadow, full of fragrant flowers. All children loved to play on the high grass of that meadow from the early morning to the sunset. They called the beautiful meadow "Pollyanna". But parents did not allow their children to go further from the meadow.

Beyond that fragrant meadow, the dark and dangerous forest had already begun. In some distance the Caucasus Mountains has been turning blue in the dawn. There were some hills close to Grandmother's house, and the vineyards were planted around the town.

When on the West the sun went down into the Black sea, it was sending farewell greetings to the mountains, and the mountains got the pink color from the sunset. Then, bizarrely, the bald part of the mountains was turning to the pink color and shimmered with the magnificent colors.

Most often in the summer, Alenushka tried to escape from the small dark house to the sunny street, or to the meadow to play with her friends. She often preferred to sit near the water stream on the street more than working in the garden. There, in a fast mountain stream, she loved to build small dams for the tadpoles. Then, she watched them turn into small frogs.

Early in the morning and in the evening, the neighbor's goats and cows were passing by to the pasture. The small bell around their necks was cheerfully ringing. They were leaving piles of manure behind them, and Grandma called her husband

Minai to collect the manure and put it under the trees to fertilize the garden. Grandfather unwillingly, and with no pleasure, did it. He always was angry at the hard working and persistent grandmother, who always worked all day long. Then, geese followed the cows and goats along the street to the meadow, passing by the playing girl. Alenushka was afraid of them. If the geese met anybody along the way, they hissed and chased people who did not want to give them the road.

Sometimes in the Summer Alenushka ran away from the strict Grandfather Gorenych, to hide in the flower nursery which was across the house. There she admired everything around, remaining invisible. Unearthly beauty of the small flowers with the name violets or pansies was striking her the most. Many of them were planted according to the shades of the flowers in the long flower beds. There was a flower row consisting only of bright yellow flowers. And the other flower bed had only dark purple violets and other colorful violets. It was all unusually joyful.

Alenushka loved to find and enjoy some beauty around her. But she was always hungry, and therefore she had the habit of trying everything for taste and smell. She really wanted to taste the violets too. But they were so beautiful, joyful and gentle that, picking a flower, Alenushka started to caress and examine it for a long time. But hunger prevailed, and she bit off a small bite. Violets were edible and very tasty.

Despite the fact that these flowers had short stems, Alenushka picked up a few multi-colored violets and carried home to please her grandmother. But the grandmother was not happy about the flowers plucked on someone else's flowerbed. They belonged to a government nursery, and they were prohibited to be picked up.

"You could be punished for this" said her upset grandmother. *"Would you be happy if someone would take your*

own toys without asking you first? You cannot touch someone else's stuff, even if it's a very beautiful thing, and even if you really want to have it."

Actually, Alenushka wasn't allowed to pick flowers anywhere at all. Grandma said that all flowers are alive, and they also want to stay in their own home as long as possible. *"Well, here you pick a flower. And in a day it will dry up. On the other hand, in the garden we all can admire them for a long time,"*- said the kind woman. Then, she added that she was called "Pansies" in her youth. Later in life Alenushka always remembered her grandmother's lesson when she saw these flowers.

***

Pansies Tales

Alenushka saw many different flowers and herbs not only in the flower nursery, but growing in the garden, as well. Her grandmother used the herbs for the compress and made ointments for the dry skin. Alenushka had all sorts of scratches and insect bites in abundance on her skin. Grandmother treated her skin with all kinds of herbs, including violets. She also used violets as a cooling, soothing and anti-inflammatory agent. And sometimes she even sugared this plant, turning it into jam. Besides, she made tea from the dried leaves of mint or lemon grass, and put some leaves in a salad. But she warned that the roots of the violet were poison and nobody should eat them.

Alenushka especially liked the dark violets with yellowish-white petals. Grandmother said that their petals symbolized a love triangle, and told a legend about the similarity of the violet petals with the eyes of some mysterious creature.

There were many stories, paintings, art works devoted to these flowers. Russian peasants told a story about one kind and pure hearted girl Anna, who fell in love with a visiting guy. Before leaving the village, he promised to return for her, but did not keep his promise. Every day Anna went out onto the road and waited for her lover.

When she realized that she had been deceived, she had so much grief from the unrequited love that she died. Amazingly beautiful flowers with three-colored petals grew on her grave. The white color on the flower means the girl's hope for reciprocity and happiness. The yellow color means surprise that the groom does not come for a long time. The purple color means sadness from the realization of the betrayal.

One ancient myth described: "On one stuffy day, the beautiful goddess Venus decided to swim in a sheltered pond, where no one would see her. However, while bathing, she, looked back at the noise, and saw people looking at her with enthusiasm and surprise. Venus demanded that the God Zeus would punish them for spying on her. But, being in a good mood, Zeus simply turned the curious people into pansies."

***

Narcissus

During heavy rains, Alenushka spent a lot of time on the terrace looking at the window. When she saw that daffodils were blooming near the front door, she was very happy. This meant that spring had come, and soon it would be possible to go out into the yard. She loved the strong sweet smell of daffodils. Grandma also knew a lot of interesting things about these flowers. She said that the English call daffodils "spring lilies."

Alenushka wanted to know more about the flowers, especially after her grandmother told her that the great Tsar Peter I brought some daffodils to Russia. The name of Tsar Peter-Enlightener was well known to the girl. The grandmother read her the "Battle of Poltava" by Pushkin, where Peter the Great defeated the Swedes.

"The word 'narcissus' has the same root as the word 'anesthesia' because the plant has a sweet, intoxicating smell," - her grandmother Anna began the story. *The smell of the daffodils is so strong and sweet they have been used since ancient times in the manufacture of perfumes."*

Alenushka and her grandmother also tried to make perfumes out of many flowers. For example, they would put rose petals in a small bottle of alcohol. But for some reason, they did not succeed in the daffodil perfumes. Apparently, there was another secret to it. One evening, before going to bed, the grandmother told her granddaughter an ancient legend.

"Once upon a time in Ancient Greece there were many gods. And there lived a handsome young man named Narcissus. He was indifferent and cold to people. He was not interested in their opinions and did not need anyone to be with him. He loved and constantly admired himself. Once, one beautiful nymph fell in love with this young man. But he did not answer her with any emotions but even ridiculed her being in love and did it in an offensive and rude form. In those days, love was considered a great feeling, and mockery of it belonged to the category of the biggest sin.

Insulted by Narcissus' laughter, the beautiful goddess Aphrodite decided to punish the handsome but egoist person. One hot day the young man was on the hunt and wanted to drink water from a stream. But suddenly he saw the face of a charming young fellow in it and fell in love with him. Although his own reflection was looking at him, Narcissus could not take his eyes off the beautiful reflection. With wild passion, he fell to the surface of the water, wanting to kiss the reflection. He had neither the strength nor the desire to move away from the water. In the end, his divine body disappeared, and at this place, a no less beautiful flower blossomed. This flower came to be called a daffodil. It became associated with deceptive desires and selfishness."

All kinds and all parts of daffodils are poisonous and animals never eat them. Also, it is better no to add them to bouquets with other colors because of the toxic substance in them. The Greeks called it the flower of death, and they have never presented it as a gift to loved ones. *"Please, do not touch them, don't cut these flowers, and don't bring them to the house. You could just admire and smell them in the yard,"* once more said wise grandmother.

***

Chamomiles

There were many wild daisies and chamomiles growing on the meadow near the grandmother's house, and children loved to play there. The girls gathered the daisies and cornflowers making bouquets, or they made wreaths from the flowers to dress their heads, like crowns. They also were fortune telling by the daisies' petals, tearing one at a time and saying "loves, doesn't love."

Alenushka loved daisies, chamomiles, cornflowers and many other wild flowers. She also enjoyed being with her friends on that beautiful meadow.

Grandma Anna often called Alenushka to go to the meadow to collect some herbs. Then she dried them and made some medicine. The good Fairy Anna knew well the healing properties of various herbs, and how to treat people with them. The neighbors called her "a healer." She often brewed chamomile tea, successfully using this tincture as a sedative and antibacterial tea. Grandmother, believing in the miraculous power of the plant, used this chamomile tea to treat inflammation of the gastrointestinal tract and during colds. It is interesting that the grandmother treated herself with chamomile, as she had high acidity. She recommended drinking chamomile broth to neighbors with any stomach ailments and had been treating her husband who had an ulcer. She also often suggested young mothers to make a bath with the chamomile tea and wash their small children in it.

Once Alenushka learned about the usefulness of chamomile, she decided to start to collect this wonderful herb in order to hand it over to the pharmacy, earn some money and help her grandmother. One morning she spent on collecting huge amount of these medicinal flowers. However, dried flowers have shrunk in size and in weight. Nevertheless, Alenushka took them to the town pharmacy which was very far from the grandmother's house. Finally, the young girl came to the pharmacy, happily carrying her big bag with the dried chamomiles. But behind a counter

she met an unsmiling, stern woman. The pharmacist said that she would take only the very dry chamomiles and would pay for it by its weight. Alenushka was very disappointed about the tone of that unfriendly voice and the negative attitude of the pharmacist. Also, the meager pay seemed unfair and disproportionate to the enormous work that the girl put into it. Alenushka was disappointed by the result she got, and after this incident she did not collect herbs for the purpose of "profit."

***

When you help people while doing charity (once grandma said), it gives you an opportunity to show your best human qualities:selflessness, kindness, and love for one's neighbor.

Alenushka wanted to be useful helping people. In life, nothing passes without a trace, but is intertwined and connected by some invisible threads. Alenushka had deep knowledge about ancient folk remedies and wanted to use it for people's benefits. A few decades later, in the dashing 1990s Russia did not have good medicine. At that time Alenushka lived in St. Petersburg and was a business woman. Soon after "Perestroika" she opened her own pharmacy of medicinal herbs.

***

Ancient Dolmen

One summer morning, Grandfather Minai decided to climb to the top of the Morhotsky ridge. He wanted to find out if there are the ancient and absolutely amazing structures there, as some people told him. Wherever grandfather went out of the house, the suspicious grandmother Anna always insisted that he would take Alenushka with him. At such moment, he became angry and stubborn. But the curious Alenushka promised that she would not complain or whine if she got tired.

Of course, the first thing Grandfather Minai took with him was his old camera. He never parted with it while walking around the town. It was his only friend, his entertainment and hobby. He devoted all his time to photographing and printing pictures in his hidden place behind the house. While he was getting ready, the caring grandmother cooked "Jacket Potato" in a pot. Then, she wrapped a piece of bacon in a clean fabric, put some salt in the matchbox, and added some brown bread and one onion. That was all that they had in the house. For Alenushka, loving grandmother wrapped two fresh carrots from the garden and poured some healing, fresh well water in a flask.

Alenushka often watched her grandmother work and listened to what she was murmuring. Therefore, she immediately asked: *"Why do you call that "Jacket Potato" or a "potato in uniform?" It does not have a coat or a fur coat. It is not a boss and not a military man like Grandfather Minai."* But the grandmother patiently replied that it is a metaphor. The color of the peel of the boiled potato resembled the color of the grandfather's uniform. And also, some time ago, he ate such potato with his soldiers in the war.

"In fact," her grandfather added, *"The Suvorov soldiers gave this name during the war of 18th century. They baked potatoes in the ash and joked that potatoes were also soldiers."*

Alenushka later decided to definitely ask her grandfather more about who those "Suvorov's soldiers" who baked potatoes in the jackets in the ash. Maybe she needs to become one such soldier, as well? Then, she began to repeat it to herself that she would not forget it: "Ask grandfather about the legendary Russian general Suvorov, ask about the Suvorov."

Grandmother Anna carefully packed food in the old camping bag. She did not pay much attention to her well-read husband's caustic comment. But at the same time, she taught her granddaughter, out of habit:

"Alenushka! As you get tired in the mountains, sit on a stump and eat potatoes in their skins. It is not only tasty but also healthy. It protects against infectious diseases and viruses."

Then Alena again wanted to ask the numerous questions that she always had inside her mind. The questions were strewed like peas from her. But her grandmother hurried her, saying that her grandfather did not like to wait. There, he was at the gate already, and Alenushka ran after her grandfather.

***

Finally, they were walking to the mountains together, as Alenushka dreamed, and walked for a long, long time. The sun already was high above their heads soaring hot. Alenushka had a hat on her head which her kind Aunt Dusya presented girl some time ago. And Grandfather Minai had his round skullcap on his bald skull. Soon, they were so far up, that they even passed the inscription "Lenin with Us." Alenushka knew that Lenin was the leader of the Bolshevik revolution of 1917 and overthrew the tsar. She liked the Russian tsars, and she did not like Lenin. The inscription was huge, done by the rocks, painted by white paint. Usually every year, pioneers from the school were sent to do that job.

Well, finally, they climbed the mountain. Alenushka

 looked down, and saw that all around seemed like in a magical fairy tale. There was the whole city and the bay of

the Black sea in full view. The bay looked like a frying pan with a handle, where the handle went into the open sea. Alenushka was happy to see all of it, and wanted to stand there for a long time and admire such a wonderful sight.

But then the girl began to look for a stump to sit on it, relax and have a bite with what her grandmother gave them on the road. However, the food was in her grandfather's bag, and he walked further and further, without looking back. So, Alenushka again ran after him, barely catching a breath. With her all last strength, Alenushka trailed behind the ruthless grandfather. Suddenly, a huge stone structure covered with moss opened to them. It was evident that most of it had long gone into the ground. But still that strange construction looked impressive and scary, like the house of Baba Yagi from Pushkin's fairy tale.

"Here we are. This is the mysterious Dolmen," - said the grandfather with importance in his voice.

There were two holes at the corners of the top plate of the Dolmen. It looked as thousands of years ago someone had a huge mechanism with levers. The ancient, strong heroes inserted the levers into the holes, lifted the huge stone up, closing the room on the top. It was simply unbelievable that many centuries ago someone had the amazing ability to cut huge stones so smoothly and correctly, creating a vault or a religious burial. Also, this ancient structure had a completely round hole in the center. And the same round lid from the entrance, like a bottle cork, was lying nearby.

Alenushka immediately looked inside, but she was afraid to step in there. Anyway, it was empty long time ago. However, a monstrous force and terrible secrets from the powerful structure blew at her. The girl thought that such a strong Dolmen house was inaccessible up in the mountains. It was a powerful fortress, or crypt. Nobody knew for sure what it was.

"That's how it should be built - for ages," she thought, recalling how her grandmother scolded Minai for a poorly built stove, which did not give much heat in the winter. When Minai put some wood into it, the stove always was smoking making their house very uncomfortable. Here on the top of the Mountain near the Dolmen, the air was fragrant and fresh, and they enjoyed incredible view around them. The grandfather Minai immediately began to photograph that shocking structure and everything that he saw around. Since Alenushka was not interrupting, but carefully listening to him, rejoicing grandfather continued to reveal his deep knowledge to her. *"Here, on the top of the Caucasus Mountains, you can find several such unique structures - Dolmen, like this one here. Obviously, the blocks of stones weigh thousands of kilograms. But look how beautifully they were carved and still stand upright. Look, the space above is covered by another huge slab".*

Suddenly, to the left of this Dolmen Alenushka saw a bush of her beloved wild blackberry. She was very surprised to see these bushes grew so merrily high in the mountains. But first, she glanced at her strict grandfather, who always prohibited her everything. She was always afraid of him, but now her grandfather was silent, looking down at the town.

Alenushka glanced at the silent chilling Dolmen and asked his permission to get the berries. Suddenly Dolmen whispered: *"You must go to your goal through all thorns…"* And Alenushka immediately rushed to the prickly bushes to collect such healing and juicy berries. Despite the nettles, the eternally hungry girl began to eagerly pick up tasty black and some completely immature red berries, ignoring the thorns of some weeds. These amazing berries were as tasty as in the ditch near the house of her beloved grandmother Anna. These berries near the Dolmen saved Alenushka from hunger and restored her strength.

Grandfather Minai finally stopped taking pictures and took out the bag of food. Alenushka looked around, but did not see the wooden log to sit on, that grandmother was talking about. She perched next to her grandfather on the grass. Everything that a loving grandmother put on the road was incredibly tasty.

Alenushka was chewing her little food and thinking, that in

order to achieve something important in life, she must overcome all obstacles. Those thoughts gave her a lot of strength, and she could go back down the mountain to her grandmother's poor house to live her life and dream about a beautiful future.

***

The next day Minai went to his secret hut, hidden behind the house and started to make his new photos. Sometimes Alenushka was allowed to go there too, and she studied the skills of photographing. It was the old technique of fixing photos in a special chemical solution, film development and drying them after that.

Later, on the photo with the Dolmen, Minai wrote: *"Gelendzhik. The ancient stone house of the heroes."* Grandfather used a pre-revolutionary font for the inscriptions in his photographs. He had a set of tiny printed letters of the entire old alphabet. Sometime in the late 1950s, he bought this set of printed letters in the market along with the unique albums of old Gelendzhik. These priceless photographs belonged to the famous Gelendzhik photographer Alexander Krivonos, who lived in the city until the 1930s.

***

Important Bubbles

The wonderful cat Murka lived with Alenushka on the top of the stove. Cat often told her: *"Strive to the moon! Even if you don't get there, you will still find yourself among the stars"*. Alenushka really wanted to get to the stars and tried to understand how to do it. But her cat Murka did not say more about it.

According to Russian tradition, children often arranged various entertainments for guests. The task of the parents was to demonstrate the cultural knowledge and talent of the children. It was a tradition, some kind of an exam, and the duty of any child to sing a song or read a poem when guests were invited for a dinner. Usually, a short children's concert was happening during a dessert.

However, there were never any guests in the house of Grandfather Minai before. Only once, during Christmas, he invited his new acquaintances to the house. Grandmother was putting all her effort into the cooking dinner with little food they had at home. But her main pride was her little granddaughter, who knew different poetries in countless numbers. Before that evening, Grandfather approached Alenushka and ordered her to behave decently, not to indulge, and not to ask any questions during their dinner. Then, in a slightly softened voice, he added that she could read poetry.

It was evident that the Grandmother was concerned, as well. She cleaned their rundown house, washed the dishes, and scrubbed the smoked glass of a kerosene lamp. At the same time, she was murmuring under her nose to herself.

"Some unknown fools soon will visit us, and my Alenushka should amuse them. I know for sure, they will sit like "blown bubbles" and would be silent, like at their own funeral."

The little child did not understand the meaning of those strange words but tried to memorize them and use later. After the modest meal, her grandfather put a chair in the center of the room, like a tribune, and strictly called for the granddaughter. Alenushka climbed up in the chair and examined the room. She was a very sensitive girl, who was accustomed to observing everything around her, quickly understanding the mood, or even psychology, of adults. The unsmiling faces looking at her with cold impatience took her aback. In the arrogant faces of the wives of these officials, Alenushka saw some doubt in her ability to make a good impression or to recite verses or say something worth their precious attention.

Those cold people embarrassed her, and she had no desire to give them her gift of performing or share with them her talent. But the inner fear of being punished by her grandfather overcame her confusion. The little girl gathered all her courage, inhaled the air to sound louder (as her grandmother taught her), and blurted out:

"Well, here I am with a concert! Why are you silent, like the blown bubbles at your own funeral? Clap as you supposed to do in a real theater!"

Then, she happily and triumphantly glanced at her Grandmother, seeking her approval, rejoicing at her own ingenuity. But deathly silence was the answer to the little girl. At the same time, the eyes of Grandmother, for some reason, were grimly lowered down and did not sparkle with joy, as Alenushka expected. Then, in certain consternation, the girl looked at her Grandfather. He was the one who taught her to speak clearly and loudly, and not to mumble something under her nose. But with the terrifying feelings, she saw his very red and angry face.

This was probably not the best start they all expected from his granddaughter.

Alenushka was terribly afraid of her tough Grandfather. She did not want to end this night in a dark corner with her knees on the pea beans. But the face of Grandfather told her that he plans to put her there very soon. The girl was feverishly thinking about how to fix the menacing situation very quickly and smartly. She desperately tried to recall all the funny stories from all fairy tales, and how their heroes came out of the most difficult problems. Therefore, in order to take time and fearing Grandfather's punishments, she began to bow to all other directions. She was trying to flatter these cold, uninvited, pompous to guests, "as the blowing balloons", as her Grandmother accidentally mentioned it in front of her recently.

Then, suddenly, some funny words from a radio program came to her mind. Almost hysterical from the fear, but trying to choose the words without the "R" (which she could not pronounce), Alenushka began almost to scream louder and clearly: "*Dear listeners! Here I am, the Great Actress Kanyakula!*"

And she again bowed to these "puffed-up silent bubbles

filled with of foolishness," who with frowned faces gazed silently at her, judging shaking their heads in condemnation.

Alenushka felt very uncomfortable from her own deep bows. But still, she began to read to them what they expected, a very well-known and politically correct poem: "*Stone is to stone. Brick is to brick. Our Lenin died, Vladimir Ilyich. We are still young, but we are gaining more strength. The party of Stalin and the party of Lenin forbade punish us.*"

This politically correct poem glorifying their communist's leaders seemed to them a good and relevant one. They began to laugh and to clap a little. But still, they could not resist the teachings her grandparents, saying:

"*You have to keep your granddaughter in strong hands, or, as people say, in 'porcupine mittens.' She and your family are not far from some troubles*".

Grandfather frowned and barely was holding his temper, but was silent and did not look at the grim guests. The grandmother was silent for a while, as well. Then, she said under her own nose that she does not want to share her last piece of the black bread with anybody ever again. And Alenushka was ashamed of the ignorance and cruelty of these guests. She ran away, but then came back and began to look into the keyhole, deciding whether to wait for her punishment or not.

Grandmother began to give some tea to the guests. She apparently was pleased that her granddaughter made these grim guests laugh by playing the clowning game and "saving all their faces," as she noticed later. Encouraged, Alenushka went out to the guests again, and began to recite her favorite verses:

"At Lukomorye the oak is green; the golden chain is on that oak. Day and night, the scientist cat goes around the chain. "

Despite her very young age, Alenushka had an extraordinary memory and knew by heart almost the entire thick book of well-known Pushkin's poems. She could spend hours reading them. It was her real great joy. But the guests did not want to listen to her beloved poet at all. They were drinking and made a lot of discussion and noise with each other. Her grandfather never was drinking alcohol. He also saw that the guests were rude and not respectful to anybody in his own house. But at the beginning of 1950's, the situation in the country was very dangerous and unstable, and he could not say a word to his rude guests.

And the girl at that moment sensed that she was very smart, but also she was chained to an imaginary oak tree, as a cat in the Pushkin poem. Her only consolation was that in that evening for the first time she performed not under her own name. But she was an actress with her own pseudonym, and nobody would punish a performing actress. She was happy with her discovery while acting like a famous actress Kanyakula who was allowed some scenic liberties. But she was still sad. In that evening she felt as if she had already lived a long and difficult life. She sadly went to her cold bed incredibly tired, having experienced tremendous stress while looking for a way out of a difficult situation. Her Grandfather never invited anybody to his house again.

In 1953 Stalin died, his statues were removed from everywhere, and later, Lenin's sculptures were put away from all cities, as well.

***

Carry your Sleigh

Time passed. Grandfather gradually got used to the little girl who lived in his house from her birth. He even became interested in answering her many different questions. Sometimes he taught Alenushka to play chess, to take photos and develop the photographs with him in his secret room. The other time, under the pressure and insistence of his suspicion wife he took Alenushka with him to the town where he usually took a lot of pictures. Then at his secret room behind the house, in the dark, he developed and fixed the film, and printed his countless photographs. Alenushka, too, was very interested in all his activities and learned how to patiently help him.

At the end of December, Grandfather decided to go to the forest and bring a Christmas tree. Alenushka begged him to take her with him, and the grandfather reluctantly agreed. He took a gun, a sleigh, called for dogs and went to the forest. It seemed that the forest was not so far, but the day before, surprisingly deep snow suddenly fell and it was difficult to walk. At first the dogs dragged the sleigh, but soon they got tired, and Minai released them into the wild. Then Grandfather instructed the girl to drag the wooden sleigh and gave her the ropes from the sleigh. At this day Alenushka learned on practice the well know Russian proverb *"If you like to ride the sleigh, you have to carry the sleigh."*

Alenushka had never yet had a sleigh ride. Usually, the weather in Gelendzhik was mostly warm, and snow rarely fell. So Grandfather had to explain to her that this proverb meant: any reward requires labor first. And then they went further.

They walked for a long time. And then, finally, they entered the dark forest and found the clearing where there was a stump. First, the grandfather began to teach Alenushka to shoot a gun. But that weapon was too big for her. But the grandfather also had with him his small revolver, as well, and he helped the little

girl learn to use it. The recoil of the shot reflected in her shoulder, and she fell down. Minai laughed and said another proverb: "*hard in the learning, but easy in the battle.*" He was very smart and well-read.

On that day he was very glad to be outside on the snow and teach his granddaughter something useful (as he thought). Also, he did not have his wife nearby who always was buzzing like a bee. Therefore Minai was in a good mood. Then, he unfolded his food and began to eat. Alenushka was hungry as well but did not like to eat his salted pork with the garlic. She just chewed some bread and washed it down with some water. But when Grandfather turned away, she grabbed two small pieces of the pork and threw it to the dogs. They happily quickly swallowed the food. Then they again looked at the girl with devoted eyes and thanked her, waving their tails:

"We always remember your kindness, Alenushka. There will be a day when we will show you our gratitude, too!"

Grandfather finished his lunch, looked around, and cut down one small and prickly tree. Rather, it was just a juniper bush or some other evergreen bush. Then, Grandfather put the tree on the sled and ordered Alenushka to drag it home. But it was beyond her strength. Then, Grandfather harnessed the dogs to the sled and began to whip them. The girl immediately grabbed the rope of the sled, helping the dogs to drag the heavy sled with the Christmas tree. A few steps later, she saw the cat Murka walking towards them. The cat Murka, who was a Fairy, also helped them to pull the sled on the snow. So, with her help, they all returned home together.

When they came back, the house was already warm. Grandmother was cooking potatoes in the skin. After the dinner, cat Murka jumped to the top of the stove, and Alenushka climbed up after the cat. They hugged and fell asleep soundly. At night, when Grandfather fell asleep and snored, Grandmother put the Christmas tree in a bucket with water. And then she strengthened it on all sides with the pieces of wood so that the tree would not fall. And then she took out several colorful toys from the chest, some iridescent tinsels, paper patterns in the form of snowflakes, and hung it all on the Christmas tree. Then she threw some pieces of fluffy cotton on the fluffy branches that it would look like snow. Grandma Anna was making this beauty and thought: *"There will be a holiday for Alenushka here when she would wake up."*

Grandmother was a Kind Fairy and could do everything. She put a little bag under the Christmas tree with a present, which she had prepared in advance. There were two walnuts in that bag, which Grandmother painted with a golden color, and two delicious cookies. But most importantly, Grandmother put there two long-prepared orange and fragrant tangerines there. *"Here, Alenushka will be delighted*!" And the cat, Murka, also wanted to become an ornament of this tree and to please Alenushka. Cat went down from the stove, climbed the Christmas tree, and hid there until the morning. Cat Murka sits there and thinks:

"Alenushka will wake up and call me. And I will not show up and do not respond immediately, but will hide and play with the girl! "

***

Carnival

One day, just before the New Year, suddenly the mother Emma came to visit her parents and the girl. She said that she would take Alenushka to a children's costume party. But Alenushka did not have any costume to go to the carnival. Then the mother went to her boss Bella Naumovna and brought an old "snowflake costume" because Bella's daughter had a new one. Grandmother tried to renew and starch it. But something went wrong; the tutu did not dry well and looked awful. But Alenushka was nevertheless dressed up in that costume which had a slightly grayish color. They all went to the celebration in the town. Despite everything, Alenushka was very proud of her first trip to the world.

By tradition, in order to receive a gift from Grandfather Frost children should have read poetry, sang songs, or danced. Alenushka knew many different poems, short and long, and loved to perform for the audience. The most beloved and simple rhymes were done by the poet Agnia Barto. It was easy to remember. When Grandmother read a book to the girl, she imagined the pictures of what she was reading about. She also lamented, empathized, and worried together with the characters of the books.

"I love my horse; comb her hair and her tail. On the horseback I will ride." or *"The mistress forgets about her old bunny outside in the rain. The rabbit was small and could not get off the bench."* Sometimes Alenushka thought that she, too, was an abandoned bunny, and she felt sad.

On the eve of the carnival, Grandmother Anna was worried and tried to prepare Alenushka for the upcoming ball as well as possible. She repeated various poems with her, trying to choose the most spectacular, so as not "to smash her face" in front of the public and authorities.

***

A Christmas tree for the employees of KurortTorg was arranged on the second floor of the "House with Tower" ("On the Roof"). That well-known building in Gelendzik was near the port, on the corner of Lenin Street. When mother Emma and Grandmother Anna finally reached that place, they saw that the evening was already in full swing.

Around the Christmas tree was already crowded with many children in a variety of wonderful costumes. Their parents stood behind them also in beautiful clothes. Most boys were dressed in bunnies and bears costumes. Alenushka suddenly saw that there were many girls in similar white tutus as she had. Only their snowflake costumes were well ironed and beautifully decorated with sparkles. Many costumes looked fantastically airy and magnificent, with embroidery, sequins, and fancy bead patterns. In addition, many girls had very beautiful crowns. The crowns had glittering fragments of small Christmas decorations glued to them and sparkled with colorful lights. Some of these dressed-up rich girls even had makeup on their lips and cheeks (according to a sharp remark of the grandmother).

Alenushka also dreamed about the attention, approval, and praise, which she did not get at home at all. She tried joyfully smiling at everything around her, not wanting to notice the slanting looks and whispering of the people around her. But she had the look of Cinderella, who nevertheless managed to get out to the ball, but without a festive outfit. It was as if she had been pushed onto a Christmas tree in the old and already unnecessary dress of her older sister. But Alenushka was not envious. No matter what, she was very happy to see all this New Year's beauty.

After the cold, cramped and dark house, lit by only one kerosene lamp, Alenushka could not take her eyes off this New

Year's magic. At the Christmas tree, Showgirl and Santa Claus led a round dance with the children, in which the mother also tried to push her daughter. And, in the end, Alenushka took a chance and went to them. But for some reason, the children did not give her a hand. Alenushka suddenly found herself in the middle of a huge room among the prickly looks of strangers. Children continued to walk around the beautiful Christmas tree and sing: *"A Christmas tree was born in the forest, and it grew in the forest. In winter and summer, it always was green."*

For many years this popular song was accompanied every Christmas Party, as a symbol of the New Year. Alenushka knew the words of that song, but what was the point of her singing alone? Well-dressed children did not let her in their circle of the dance. Seeking consolation, Alenushka sadly went back to her loved ones. But her mother even before that event was most often very restrained and even strict with her. She never stroked the girl's head, hugged her, and never spoke her kind words. This time, mother Emma was especially angry with Alenushka; she did not take the hand of her daughter seeking support.

Then the time came for the concert. The children began

taking turns to go out to the center, read poems, and receive gifts for this. Then the turn for Alenushka came to go there and speak. She decided to do it quickly and began to speak vigorously: *"Our Tanya cries loudly: she dropped a ball into the river. Hush, Tanya, don't cry: The ball will not drown in the river."*

But when she glanced into the hall, she was very embarrassed and even upset by the disrespectful noise. Then she took in a little more air, as her grandfather taught her and loudly declared her favorite poem by Pushkin, the best poet of all time: *"At the Lukomorye the oak is green! The Golden chain is on that oak".*

But nobody listened to her and the noise and laughter grew. Alenushka very much loved the romantic and tender poet Pushkin. She did not want to shout louder trying to overcome the noisy crowd. Then she sighed again, gathered her strength, and decided to defeat everyone with strong poet Nekrasov. She closed her eyes to concentrate, and with the threatening intonations, in the lowest voice she could be capable of, slowly and distinctly began to recite:

"There is not the wind rage over the forest, nor are the

streams running from the mountains. It is the Grandfather Frost walks around, inspecting his possessions. He looks: - are the forest trails well drifted, and are there cracks, crevices, and where is the bare land?"

The poem was long and very difficult. But Alenushka believed that her artistic talent would triumph over everything. She continued to recite with effort, feeling growing furious anger at the whole world unfair to her. Her performance was the last one. The children were tired of a long evening and were expecting only gifts. After the second verse upset, offended little girl just ran away again, seeking solace in her mother's arms.

"I will not read anything else for these fools. I don't need their handouts, their pathetic little present. I'll live without everything, as before. I don't need anyone's love", she muttered bitterly. But her mother had a different opinion. Instead of consoling the little girl in her grief, Emma began to shame and to scold her. Then Alenushka looked at her Grandmother, who always helped and protected her in difficult situations. But Grandma looked the other way apologetically smiling to the boss Bella Naumovna as if making excuses after the granddaughter.

Alenushka thought that if she would now cry, then they will take her away from the Christmas tree carnival, which was nevertheless so attractive to her. But around Alenushka there was such a deep vacuum of loneliness that she bit her lips strongly in the effort not to cry. Instead, she forced herself to laugh. From now on, she always was laughing during strong distress, as a protection for her innocent and fragile soul.

Soon even worse came. The organizers began to choose some children in the best costumes, and send them to Santa Claus in the middle of the room. There they were taking some photos with other beautifully dressed children, a showgirl, and Santa. Alter that, all were given attractive little bags with something amazingly tasty inside. But Alenushka was not invited to Santa Claus and was not given a gift. She felt even more and more bitter. But then the smiling director of KurortTorg Bella Naumovna came up to them. Bella sadly saw that Emma did not have time, money or effort to improve the old Snow tutu for Alenushka. Also, she saw that the little girl was forgotten by all around her, and did not get any gift. Bella took a small Christmas bag with some candies from her own daughter Alla and gave it to Emma's daughter. The girl immediately looked inside the gift bag. Inside the wonderful bag, there were several chocolates glittering attractively. Like many other girls, Alenushka collected colorful candy wrappers. But she did this, for the most part, wandering around all sorts of ditches on the street. So that evening she was especially nice to get the real chocolates in beautiful wrappers. There were also three tangerines there in the bag, a real luxury for winter time of their town. These mysterious, bright, juicy fruits have always been an unattainable dream of all children at that time.

At that evening, still sobbing and worried about her failure, Alenushka immediately began to regale herself with a tangerine, which also had an amazing taste. From that evening, she always loved the smell of citrus. Tangerines became a symbol of her childhood. But they only appeared in Gelendzik stores in the winter, and were always too expensive for Grandmother to buy.

That evening of her distant childhood, she sadly realized that the mood and attitude of her relatives towards her were changing depending on what some boss Bella had to say. Then Alenushka decided that she needed to stay away from all her mother's bosses and to recital her poems only at the home holidays, which were very rare.

Also, she decided that if she finally would grow up despite of all her troubles and hunger, and suddenly she would have her own children, then she would make them the most wonderful New Year's costumes, so that they would not be shy to recite poems by the Christmas tree, receive gifts from Santa Claus and take pictures with a Showgirl. Only one time more Alenushka received stimulus New Year's gift of tangerines in Moscow when she traveled there with her grandmother. But a story about it will come later.

Only one more time Alenushka received accidently a New Year's gift of tangerines in Moscow where she traveled with her grandmother. In her poor, socialist childhood no one, even in a dream, could have imagined that sixty years later Alenushka would live on a ranch in California and wander around her husband's citrus plantations. And delicious and refreshing tangerines will simply roll around under her feet, and the squirrels will eat them.

***

Kind Stove

Everybody has somewhere a special, beloved place where it is pleasant to return, even in dreams. This place for Alenushka was her grandmother's huge stove, on top of it she often was sleeping with her cat Murka.

This old-fashioned stove occupied almost the entire room. It had a small space at the top, which Grandma was calling a couch. Cat Murka considered this place to be her own, although from time to time she was glad to share it with the little girl who played with the cat there. Alenushka spent most of the cold time on the stove, sometimes falling asleep there.

Minai did not like and did not have any skills to do something in his own hands. He reluctantly was fulfilling one of his duties supplying the house with firewood. Also, one of his winter responsibilities was starting the fire in the stove. But there was no good shed for storing firewood in a dry condition. The coop and the barn in the yard had many large openings in the roof. Therefore, the firewood was very wet, as a rule, and did not want to catch fire right away. This is why the process of starting the stove was very long.

First, Minai took several small, thin branches and put them inside the hole of the stove. Then he opened the blower at the top of the stove for more air for the faster burn. Minai did not want to use kerosene or paper, since they were expensive. He did not allow buying kerosene more than once a month. Also, kerosene was used only for a forever sooty table lamp to light the house. Moreover, grandfather did not want to use his precious newspapers for kindling. He was subscribing to many newspapers, and kept them, collecting in a big pile by their dates. He enjoyed reading them for many hours every day. It was his main activity.

When the stubborn stove slowly flared up, the wood crackled merrily. However, some time ago, the stove was improperly built. The cold house instead of heating quickly always was filled with a huge amount of smoke first. Grandmother opened the door outside and ventilated the house, letting in the cold. Grandfather cursed but continued to sit by the stove, putting firewood into it.

Anna scolded her husband endlessly for his unwillingness to repair or do something for the house. He angrily and quickly went back to his room, away from her constant "buzzing". But soon he would go out to spend some time sitting near the stove, enjoyed watching the fire and straightening firewood with a poker. It seemed to be his only joy and entertainment in the loveless house.

In any case, the stove was the center of winter life. There was a large cooking hole with black soot in the middle of the stove, and it looked frighteningly scary to Alenushka. Grandmother gave the stove different names depending on her mood. She called it "Scarecrow" or "Ugly." But Alenushka loved the stove-

bread maker, and it didn't seem ugly to her. The big stove was her refuge and only friend. At the top of the warm stove she found comfort that she did not receive from people.

In winter little child was never allowed to go out, because she did not have warm clothes, and there was nothing to do outside anyway. However, the free spirited girl did not enjoy the small, closed, dark space of the house. It gave her the feel of winter captivity, and she spent most of her time on the top of the stove waiting for the arrival of spring. From time to time, mostly in the summer her mother could suddenly appear. But she did not spend much attention to the girl and soon was disappearing again for a long time. Then, Alenushka told her cat Murka: *"Maybe the magic stove will come to life one day and would take me to Sakhalin Island to my mother? That would be great! "*

She believed in the fairy tales. After all, her grandmother read her a fairy tale about a man, Ivan, who rode everywhere on the stove, like on a horse.

On long winter evenings, Alenushka often sat with her beloved grandmother at this huge steaming stove. They quietly hummed Old Russian songs. And outside the windows, the northeast wind echoed them, howling with anguish. That strong wind was tearing up their favorite apricot trees and breaking down the tender, thin branches of the cherries. It was a typical of Gelendzhik winter wind called "Nord-Oost."

In the spring, Grandma whitened the huge old stove with the lime and chalk. The stove was white, fresh, smelled pleasant and rejoiced at the cleanliness. The stove enjoyed its clean look until the next winter. In the summer, Grandma cooked all food in a small, stuffy room on the other side of the house, using kerosene. Since it was expensive, the family ate very little cooked food, but they ate all that the garden would provide.

Grandma dreamed of a good stove, and often asked her husband to build the new one. But Minai didn't want to hire a special stove-maker, saying that it was "an extra waste of his money." Generally, he did not like to spend his money for anything at all, because he was the only one who had a military pension. Grandma never worked outside her house, first raising her three children, going through World War II, and then raising her granddaughter. She did not earn any pension. *"Grandfather is greedy for every penny,"* often complained Grandma.

She really begged him every week for the grocery money before going to the store. Then she would go to the market with tears of resentment and humiliation to buy something most necessary. She often said out loud: *"After all, I should cook, clean and feed him. But he never expressed any gratitude."*

Grandfather preferred to collect and keep his money in a "safe place ".

He usually he put his metal money in the big jars and hid them in the garden soil. However, several years later his grandson found some of them there while digging the garden. But it was worth nothing at that time after the socialistic reforms of 1950's when the money depreciated (devaluation occurred). They were worth nothing, and could not help anybody to live better any more.

***

Toys

There was nobody in the grandmother's house who paid special attention to the girl, who would buy gifts for her, or who would be spoiling the little child. Alenushka did not have toys, except for one old doll Marfushka who had special meaning for her. That doll was keeping tender memory about her father Konstantin, about his beautiful eyes looking at the child with kindness. When Alenushka was several months old, Konstantin visited her in the old house where she lived with her mother Emma. Despite her young age, the child remembered that there was a very strong flood on that day. Her mother was very upset being helpless and was fighting with Konstantin. They separated forever on that day.

After that Alenushka almost never saw her father but missed him very much. Her Russian relatives did not allow him any visits or contacts with the child. Grandmother Anna always called Konstantin a Greek Demon. That sad father's doll spent most of her time with Alenushka on the top of the stove or near by the window. The doll looked sadly at what was being done outside, and almost never played with Alenushka.

When Minai was not at home, Alenushka approached the only window of the house, which was in his room. There, in Grandfather's room by the window she and her only doll were watching how endless autumn rains were pouring. They watched how trees were bending under a severe hurricane and how the puddles bubbled. Grandmother told her that if bubbles appeared in the puddles, then the rain would last long.

One day, Alenushka got another, very large German doll. This doll was given her by Grandmother's son Adik, who was a sailor. The doll was smart as a princess, and her big blue eyes moved from side to side and were closing depending on the position of the head. Also, when Alenushka moved her up and down the doll speak "ma-ma." Having an incredible curiosity, Alenushka wanted to know the doll's secret, and what was inside her. Therefore, when nobody was watching the girl, she took this doll apart. But finding nothing interesting inside it, Alenushka was very disappointed. After this experiment, she was not able to put the doll back in its previous condition and simply hid it from the eyes of the adults in order to avoid punishment. But soon the grandmother found the wreckage of the doll and was very upset about the lost beauty.

"It is normal that everybody makes mistakes. But if you purposely break something it is bad, and often it is almost impossible to put back together. Even if we would try to glue something back, it never would be the same again. The most important in life, always first to think about what would happen after you have done something. However, even more, important

to be honest and don't hide your mistakes. Talk about it, clean your soul, and live happier." But at that moment Minai came out from his room to the noise and saw the broken doll. Instead of helping her to repair it, he grabbed his belt and hit the little girl. Alenushka fell from the blow, pain, and resentment. But his cruel punishments never stopped the curiosity of the girl, and her desire to learn everything "from the inside out".

In several days the grandmother got a special illustrated rhyming picture book "What is good and what is bad" written by Vladimir Mayakovski and read it to Alenushka. *"The little boy came to his father and asked how to tell what good behavior is and what is bad…*Father said: *The rain has fallen and passed. The sun is in full shine. It is very good for grown-ups and children. If a son is darker than night, filth over his face, it is clear this is very bad for the child's skin…"*

Alenushka memorized that book forever, and when she was in a doubt, she tried to remember wise poet Mayakovski, whom poetry later she learned more.

***

Alenushka did not have many toys, but she used her imagination to make them. She would choose something surprising from the firewood, and played with the freakish little chocks. She kept them on the top of the stove and treasured her several home-made toys. She played with them in the winter, applying her imagination, endowing them with living souls, and considering them her living friends.

Once, Alenushka stored on her stove a fragrant, thin twig that represented the memory of summer. She drew a nose and mouth on it, and talked with that "magic toy". The girl imagined that this wand had special magical powers, as in a fairy tale that her grandmother had recently read to her. She wanted to believe that if she would wave this wand and said some special, secret words, a miracle would happen. Alenushka even once dreamed that a wand would help her to bring her mother back home forever.

In October Grandma unexpectedly started to pack the luggage to go to visit some distant relatives in central Russia. Alenushka begged her grandfather not to touch her magic wand. However, when they returned home in a month, the girl did not find her favorite "magic" wand in the place where she put it. Alenushka bitterly wept, feeling the pain of loss, as if she had lost her living friend.

***

Be Smart

Grandmother had three children, one daughter Emma and two sons. One son was sailor Adik, and another one was a doctor in Moscow. Adik had a beautiful wife Dusya. They were kind to Alenushka and periodically gave her gifts. Once Dusya bought Alenushka a gift; a big, inflatable, greenish-blue, beautiful ball. That ball looked like the globe that stood in Grandfather's room, and also had some contours of the continents, covered with seas and mountains. This beautiful ball aroused the girl's imagination, entertained, and amused her.

Her Grandfather often told her that being a helpful person is the most important thing in life. To which, Grandmother answered him that she would very much like to see how he was useful in the house. The grandfather replied that he was useful to his country during The War, and has many awards and medals. It was hard to argue with that, and Grandma fell silent. Although, during The World War (1941-1945), she also worked as a nurse, saving wounded soldiers. But, about The War, she did not like to talk. Sometimes, hearing her grandfather's stories about The War, Alenushka dreamed of accomplishing feats. This was necessary in order to hear more good words of approval, which were expressed very rarely to her.

One winter evening, Grandfather started the stove. Alenushka was playing nearby with her new wonderful globe ball. Suddenly very small, bright, and very hot coal fell out of the stove. Then the adults, frightened, shouted: *"Cover it! – Put the fire out!"* At this moment Alenushka wanted to show to everybody that she was a very clever and knew how to take the initiative, as her grandfather taught. She wanted to prove herself resourceful and helpful. So, she quickly grabbed her wonderful ball and pressed it into the coal, trying to put it out. Then she solemnly, like a hero, looked around, waiting for praise. She was sure that she had accomplished the feat if saving everyone from the fire. Right now, Grandfather finally would express his well-deserved respect.

She was very young, and she did not yet know the laws of nature. In addition, to the strong desire to find out everything and try everything, Alenushka really wanted to be noticed and praised. Most of the time, the neglected girl had a great desire to be useful and feel that everybody loved her. But at that very moment she was very surprised to see how softly, how easily, the red coal slipped inside her ball and disappeared there. And suddenly she felt that her beautiful ball was compressing, as the air from it hissed out. Such an unexpected result simply shocked the girl. She cried out in despair: "Grandfather! Make the ball good back again!" But Grandfather began to giggle uncontrollably; even tears came from his eyes. Maybe he felt sorry for the ball or did he get smoke in his eyes?

- *"Oh-oh-oh-oh,"* - exclaimed the upset grandmother. Then Alenushka realized that her ball could no longer be saved. It was completely ruined. Even though no one scolded or punished her, she bitterly regretted that she did not think in advance what would happen to the ball if she would use it trying to put the fire away. Alenushka climbed up to the top of the stove sad by that event. A lost ball was a rather big punishment itself. It was

a new irreparable loss, and nothing could help to return it. After she disassembled her big doll and destroyed the inflatable rubber ball, nobody gave her gifts for a long time. And she thought things had strange properties. They often turned out to be completely different from what you expected about them. And beautiful things could be really the most fragile and quickly broken.

***

Mother's Gift

Alenushka missed her beloved mother very much, and always dreamed to have her back. The most precious gift could be only from her hands. Even though the vague image of her mother went far back into childhood, but that image lived inside Alenushkas' memory, and it was always bright, soft, and warm. Alenushka kept waiting for her and waiting, thinking that one day she would break free from the Demon Konstantin or from another one, Grigori, who then was there living with her mother in Sakhalin Island.

When sometimes her mother would come back to her parents' house, Grandfather Minai would always angrily leave the room. But Alenushka and Grandma were happy that Emma unpacked her bags and stay in the house

104

for a while. One day when her mother arrived, she took out of her suitcase a pink, soft goat and said that it was a washing sponge.

At first, Alenushka did not even believe that this was a gift for her and that she could keep it for good. She asked to hold a sponge, and for some time admired the pink goat. But after a moment, Grandma removed the wash sponge away from the girl. She said that it is not a toy, and should not be broken. Later, when the grandma occasionally took Alenushka to the public bath she washed her with that pink sponge, and Alenushka was happy, thinking about her mother.

Once summer Emma came to visit her parents' house, and Alenushka saw beautiful broch on her blouse. It was a small, phosphorus deer with a huge blue turquoise eye glowing in the dark. He had a red scarf tied as a bow. His sensitive ears listened attentively to what was ahead of him. And the touching tail rose a little up from the forks. It looked like he was running somewhere with all his strength. He was so gentle and joyful, just a very sweet baby deer. Alenushka thought that it might be a gift that her mother just forgot to give her, and cheerfully asked her mother: *"And is this a gift to me?"*

At that moment, strangely her mother put her eyes silently down and thought for a minute. Then she took off her brooch and gave it to her daughter. And Grandma said: *"You forgot to buy something simple for your own child? Now your new husband Gregory would be upset that you gave away his brooch to your daughter!"*

Small Alenushka at once and forever loved this cute baby deer, who was rushing headlong to his dream, starting from the ground by his small painted hooves. With all his might he strove  to achieve something there ahead of him in the future unknown. The girl believed that he was a part of her mother's care; it was specially chosen for her and warmed by the mother's loving heart. For her, this phosphorus broch was a symbol of the motherly love she always dreamed about.

Many years later, this brooch traveled with Alenushka everywhere. Then, it was passed on to her daughter Lila, and then it was carefully migrated into the jewelry box of her granddaughter, Marina. The broch lived long and brightly in the family, experiencing all the troubles of the hectic lives of its owners. With time he slightly faded and slowed down his run, but he did not give up. The broch "baby deer" kept his cheerfulness and often reminded the owner that any pain will pass, but love will live forever. That baby deer seemed to teach that the more love there is in the soul, the brighter and happier the life. It is important just to believe in miracles, even if they are "in a sieve." Alenushka believed in miracles fervently, and there were many of them in her life.

***

Stubborness

A black lamb was walking home along a steep mountain path. On the hunchback bridge, he met with a white lamb. The white lamb said: *"Hi, Brother, here's the thing: I can't go through the bridge here. You are standing in my way."*

The black lamb answered: *"Are you out of your mind? I came first, and will not go out of the way! "*

One shook his horns, and the other stomped his feet. But no matter how much noise they made, how strongly stomping the feet, how much they twisted their horns at each other, it was not possible to pass the narrow bridge. The sun was shining above, and the river was flowing below them. But early in the morning, two stubborn lambs drowned in the river.

So mother Emma was reading to her daughter and made special emphasizing hint that Alenushka also a stubborn lamb. However, the little girl had enough criticism from her grandfather, did not like such negative comparing from her rarely-seen mother. Besides, her life was sad enough, and she did not like any sad stories. Alenushka always was looking for a happy end in fairy tales and for more love from surrounding her adults. She could not believe that the small lambs did not give way to each other and both died. Since she did not enjoy such kind of unfairness in the stubborn lambs, Alenushka asked her mother to read again and make a better end in that

story. But her mother wanted Alenushka would learn the lesson from the story and did not feel that she should change the destiny of the stubborn lambs.

One Sunday morning mother Emma took her daughter to the resort area to see the fountain "Two Lambs" and Mini took a photo of it. Later Alenushka often returned to that fountain to recall a simple tale of the wisdom of compromises. However, for a long time, she did not know how to learn patience and flexibility, to learn that consideration and respect for others make her own life much easier.

***

Restless Wandering

Due to the irrepressible curiosity and desire for adventure, Alenushka often found herself in various dangerous situations. Sometimes this happened under circumstances that she could not foresee, avoid or change. Each fall her Grandma, who tired of domestic troubles and scandals with her husband, ran away to distant wanderings. Most of the family members lived in the center of Russia in the Smolensk provinces where the snowy and frosty winter started early. There was no one to leave Alenushka with, and Grandmother took her for the trip.

For several days they rode in an uncomfortable, stuffy and crowded train, which was pounding hard. Hoping for adventure, Alenushka gazed out the window all day. But nothing interesting happened there. Only the snow and rare black little half-filled huts were visible all the way.

In the middle of the forth night, grandmother woke Alenushka up and began to dress her in a heavy fur coat. In the darkness and cold, the half-asleep little girl did not want to move anywhere. But it was a very short stop in a quiet station and grandfather's relatives were waiting for them. They took Alenushka in their arms, put her in a sled pulled by a little horse, and went to a poor house for a night. Then, Alenushka and her grandmother moved on a sleigh from one village to another, moved from one relative to another.

One evening, in one hut everyone sat down together at the table. Somebody said that it was necessary to eat what "God sent." They brought sauerkraut diluted with water and potatoes, which was cooked directly in the peel. Alenushka was put on a trestle bed near the wall and given one potato for dinner. But the hut smelled deliciously of freshly baked, black and fragrant bread. The girl was very hangry and asked for a piece of bread with some milk. She quickly ate it all and then more cheerfully looked around. Suddenly she saw how, due to the paper that had been glued to the walls, some unknown small and almost round insects appeared. Without hesitation, they headed straight to her. Alenushka was used to playing with all living creatures and then decided to watch them. But the hostess suddenly cried out: *"Hit them quickly, these are bedbugs!"*

Alenushka never wanted to kill anyone and screamed

back: - *"No, I won't beat the poor, little bugs!"* And the bugs hid back, and Alenushka soon fell asleep.

The next morning, she woke up

completely bitten from head to toe by these terrible bugs. Her arms and legs, and in general all her skin were unbearably itchy. Grandmother, in horror at seeing the child's bitten body, began to fight and curse with the mistress of the house. The next night, Alenushka was put to bed on the lounger of their huge old-fashioned stove. The stove reminded her of the one that Grandma Anna had in Gelendzik. But this one was twice as large. There she was sheltered by a sheepskin coat, which incredibly strongly smelled of a goat. But still she quickly fell asleep. The next morning began with a terrible explosion of the bottles of homemade vodka (moonshine), which was cooked in the center of the hut. Alenushka looked down and saw many pieces of bread lying on the floor. The bread was used for this strong drink. Now the strong smell of the live sheep that were inside the hut, protected from the frost, and also everywhere the strong smell of alcohol spilled on the floor were stimulating the nose. Grandma could not stand it anymore. She quickly dressed the girl and asked to be taken to another village to another relative.

But the house of the new relative was even poorer. There was no extra bed for Alenushka and her grandmother in that house for the night. But they still needed to sleep somewhere one more night before going back to the warm and beautiful Gelendzik. Therefore they had only one choice - to return to the previous hut to spend their last night there.

***

Meeting Wolves

It turned out that the relatives and their village Alenushka and her grandmother were visiting was quite far from the previous place. Also, at that time, there were no convenient roads in Russia. In winter, sleighs, skis, or horse-drawn carts were regular village transport, because all roads were completely covered with snow. Besides, it gets dark very early in winter. Grandmother Anna with difficulty found a man who agreed to drive them back to the other village.

The charioteer was grumbling and worrying that they would not get to the other place before the night, because he had a sleigh harnessed to only one horse. The lower part of the sled almost lay on the ground and although there was some hay on the bottom of the sleigh, Alenushka felt the hardness and cold of the snow underneath her. Through the snow and wind, the horse galloped pretty quickly. Alenushka was very tired of a long and hectic day, from all kinds of travels, malnutrition, and the absence of any amenities. She closed her eyes and fell asleep immediately.

Suddenly, through a dream, Alenushka heard a piercing scream from the charioteer. She immediately wanted to see what was happening there, but the grandmother pushed her back to the bottom of the sleigh. Then, in a fit of some crazy fuss, she began to cover the girl with the hay and straws trying to hide her on the bottom of it. But there was only a small amount of hay and all her efforts were in vain. Alenushka felt that she was about to cry from resentment. But then, she was dumbfounded by her Grandmother's incredibly alarmed voice. She had never before heard such excitement and fear in it. She looked at her, about to protest, but she was even more surprised. Her kind Grandmother was holding an ax in her hand. And suddenly she somehow muttered, scared, hysterically, "*Wolves*!"

Alenushka looked around and was surprised by all the strange, nervous fuss. Despite the dank cold, the driver took off his fur coat. He stood to his full height in the fast-racing sled, and his hand with a whip beat harder and harder the poor, loudly neighing horse. Among the snowy, absolute silence and emptiness of a starry night, the non-stop-screaming charioteer looked intimidating. From his wild cries, goosebumps ran on Alenushka back. And an animal horror burst inside her from the unknown and terrible word "wolves".

"Help us!" The charioteer shouted nonstop, heartrendingly urging the frightened horse to run faster. He beat her so hard that the whistle of his whip was heard in the clear frosty air. That whistling of the long whip was mercilessly revolved over a smart animal, causing protest and pity inside the girl. The tired horse was all in foam. Her huge beautiful eyes looked somehow to the side and a little back. She was breathing heavily, almost panting, and was rushing like the wind. Feeling an imminent mortal threat, the horse did everything it could, but she was almost defeated, paralyzed by the mortal horror.

Everyone was focused on something around the sled. Alenushka wanted to understand the essence of this horrible inhuman fear of the horse and people. Her curiosity prevailed, and she rose to her feet, looking around: *I would like to see*

THIS," thought she.

There were the huge, bright, billions of constellations above them everywhere the eye would catch. Through the piercing, frosty air, Alenushka saw the whole ocean of those brilliant stars in the black sky. The constellations looked almost in the same way as the grandma showed them in the summer sky. Then, the girl looked a little lower, and saw at some distance from the sleigh some bright dots, like small stars. There were many, too, and these small, piercingly burning pairs of lights came closer and closer to the sleigh. There was nothing else around, but the charioteer was screaming deafeningly from his own horror and near, seemingly inevitable death. And suddenly Alenushka clearly saw exactly what scared everyone. The driver, grandma and the horse, with their loud wild screams, neighing and waving arms, tried to scare away the large dogs catching up with the sleigh.

Alenushka was always interested in knowing what animals were thinking. And the best way to do this was to just look them in the eye. She often did this, looking into the eyes of chickens, fish, mice, cats and everyone else who had eyes. In the most of the animals in their grandmother's yard, the eyes did not express anything. But everything was different with the dogs that always were living in their yard. Alenushka loved the dogs, feeling their reliability. One dog was called Zuna, and the other one was Tuzik. Each dog had its own special character, and they showed themselves in different ways. Alenushka often stood next to them, and the brown, clever eyes of the dogs were at the level of her head. They gullibly, kindly, with love looked at the girl, realizing that she was small and she needed to be protected. They calmly talked with each other, just by looking into the eyes, and understood each other without words. They always spoke to Alenushka and taught her their fearlessness.

However, here, the leader of the pack of wolves was the largest of all of them and a very confident one. He stubbornly was rushing towards his prey by his huge flying leaps. And with each such flight he came closer and closer to the exhausted horse. A pack of wolves was already circling around the sled, surrounding them on all sides. The wolves were already so close that Alenushka clearly saw their angry, hungry eyes and panting muzzle with the protruding tongues and dripping saliva. Then, the leader of the wolves jumped towards the horse neck with intends to block the way to a retreat. But he missed it.

The little girl tried to remember how other characters of the fairy tales she knew acted in the dangerous situations. But nothing was coming out of her mind. Then she whispered the sacred words from the tale of Mowgli: *"We are of the same blood, you and me."* But the eyes of the wolves were cold and unresponsive. Alenushka began to scream these magic words louder. But from the paralyzing fear she continued to repeat *"you and I are the same blood"*. In response, she clearly heard from the pack of wolves: *"You are the great dinner!"*

The ancient awful fear rose from somewhere inside her, and nothing could be done about it. From this strange animal

inner fear, she simply s t a r t e d yelling in horror and d e s p a i r, just like the

118

charioteer and grandmother: "*Ahhhhhhh.*"

Their horse madly was looking around in a deadly neighing. She didn't have to be urged anymore, she rushed with all her might, trying to save herself. Wild fear drove her forward towards the village. And Grandma was just sitting and sobbing, still trying to cover her granddaughter with some dirty rags, straw, hay, a sheepskin coat, and her own body. In this turmoil and under the weight of all rags, the little girl had nothing to breathe. In addition, Alenushka still wanted to see the whole dramatic denouement of what was happening. Pushing off her Grandma, she rose again, almost falling out of the rapidly rushing sleigh. The charioteer, with bulging huge eyes, reached for an ax, the only weapon that was in the sleigh. Grandma was not able to hold the ax and much less fight against the wolves. Suddenly in a distance they saw several peasants with their guns, shooting up, screaming, and running closer and closer to the sleigh. The wolves slowed down, then turned around and ran away. All were saved.

***

Painful Conscience

When World War II ended in 1945, Grandma Anna for a long time was looking for her lost family members. Only in twenty years she finally found some of them in different areas of Russia. One day before the New Year, she decided to visit her brother Fedor and his wife Zinka in Moscow. She asked her husband for some money for the train, took Alenushka, and they set off on a new journey to see her brother Fedor.

The brother Fedor and his wife Zinka lived in the very center of Moscow, on Tversky Boulevard, near the monument to Pushkin. Sometimes Grandmother went out with Alenushka to buy bread or milk and returned home strolling along that beautiful area. When she was tired, she would sit down on a bench with someone to talk, while Alenushka played in the snow with her shovel and a bucket.

There were slippery ice paths in the boulevard where children were having fun. Alenushka also enjoyed riding on the frozen puddle. But then an old woman appeared and began to sprinkle sand on the ice tracks. In addition, she was muttering something unpleasant under her breath about the kids who prevent her from working.

Alenushka did not like negative remarks or hints, and especially she could not stand any lecturing from strangers. When the old woman looked away, Alenushka tried to ride on a frozen puddle but could not do it because that sand slowed down the slip. Alenushka fell down, painfully hit her back and desperately wanted to cry from the frustration that the old woman spoiled her joy. She grabbed her little spatula, ran to the hunchbacked woman Yaga, and hit her fur coat: "*Do not touch, don't destroy my ice games*"- shouted the little girl.

The old woman spun around, wanting to spank the feisty little girl. But her Grandma saw it, ran to them and quickly took her home from the boulevard. After that, Grandma did not take Alenushka with her to the store, but left her at the apartment of her brother Fedor.

***

The new grandfather Fedor lived in a huge communal apartment with more than twenty other families. However, he had three big rooms for his own. Alenushka liked to wander along the long dark corridors of the whole flat. Sometimes, she would drop into somebody's room, trying to find company and talk about life. But the neighbors most often politely and persistently escorted the girl out of their property. It was evident that they were afraid of Grandfather Fedor. Alenushka later decided to ask someone why there is so much fear everywhere.

From the neighbors she walked to the boundless communal kitchen, where only silent and angry women were cooking something stinky. Then, she wandered back to the huge apartment of unsmiling Grandfather Fedor. He never shouted at the little girl, simply not noticing her. And this is why Alenushka was not particularly scary of him, although he spoke in a low, hoarse voice. However, Fedor nonstop was talking with his newly found sister. Usually, his voice sounded very loudly, with energy and excitement. He constantly talked about the old times before the War, describing the horrible stories he lived through out. It looked like he wanted to explain his sister or to himself why he did what he did, and wanted to find an excuse for the death of many innocent people he might have been caused.

It turned out that Grandfather Fedor once worked in the NKVD (People's Commissariat for Military Affairs). His work was to identify the enemies of the State. As it occurred, he himself dispossessed many wealthy people of their wealth and carried out their executions himself. At night, he "practically could not sleep from the remorse," as Grandma said. Grandfather Fedor jumped up screaming from the nightmares and often went out to smoke in the common corridor. But he did not have any friends there and nobody talked to him. All his neighbors were terrified of him.

***

Grandfather Fedor and his wife Zinka lived very well. They even had a small TV with a huge magnifying glass. When

everyone sat down at the table to have a supper, Alenushka was taken out to another room. It was not bad, because she could watch this small TV there. And through the huge lens one could even see the costumes of artists at their gala concerts.

In that large room, on a huge desk, there was an impressive black telephone with a disk and numbers. Alenushka never saw such a wonder, and of course she could not leave it unattended. She picked up the phone, dialed several numbers, and listened to what happened next, who would answer. One day she dialed number nine. And a pleasant automatic voice announced what time it was now. And another time, someone just started asking different questions, so the girl got scared and hung up. But soon grumpy Fedora's wife noticed these games of the child and forbade her to touch the phone.

Moreover, in that large room with a TV and telephone, there was a fragrant Christmas tree to the very ceiling. This wonderful Christmas tree was decorated with huge, shimmering balls and very elegant German toys. Of course, Alenushka wanted to touch at least one such wonderful glass toy. But suddenly the crystal ball fell to the floor, and crashed with a thin ringing into many little pieces. Immediately, the furious Zinka flew into the room. She, like a witch, sparkled with her eyes at Alenushka, and as if she was throwing lightning at a little disobedient child, and yelled: *"Well, after all, unexpectedly the starving poor relatives came here to destroy our lives."* And then Zinka wanted to spank the naughty girl, but Alenushka dodged and ran to her Grandmother.

However, this time her Grandma did not defend her, as always. To the contrary, she began extremely loudly scolding the girl. Alenushka was very upset, and decided that it was time to cry. But to everyone's surprise, and instead of the punishment, Grandfather Fedor suddenly took a gift bag from the top of a high cupboard and gave it to Alenushka. At the same time, he was murmuring something condemning not in favor of his angry wife. Zinka was very angry with him for that. She planned to give all the gifts to her own, already grown-up, son, and not to this frisky relative who came from nowhere. *"There was nothing left to do in the apartment, and general, in Moscow,"* said Alenushka to herself. And she became completely bored.

***

Elefant-Prizoner

But the next day, Grandfather Fedor decided to show them Moscow and spend some useful time. Therefore, everyone went to the zoo. Prior to this, Alenushka did not know what a ZOO was. But it turned out that it was a prison for animals that were caught some time ago, but not killed completely.

Also, for Alenushka who loved animals, the whole visit to that zoo was rather unpleasant due to the dirt and bad smell there. Most of all, the girl was worried about the animals and birds in small cages. She was used to seeing them in her grandmother's magical garden, freely and cheerfully fluttering, enjoying a free life. And here they all clearly were suffering. However, for some reason this fact did not occur to adults. They tried somehow to artificially be surprised and admired all they saw, looking at the snakes behind the glass, sited under an electric lamp. And then they pointed at the eyes of the crocodile that was swimming in the very small, closed pool.

But suddenly attention of the girl was attracted by a huge and rather skinny elephant. He barely fitted in a very small cage, which was cleaned by a man, probably his master or caretaker. The elephant apparently was very hungry. The cleanliness of his small cage was not important to him. He clearly would have preferred to chew something delicious. Also, he obviously dreamed to get out to the freedom and live in the vast jungle

Then Alenushka crept closer to his cage and threw him her

precious tangerine from grandfather Fedor present. The elephant was very surprised and looked at Alenushka with an intelligent eye. And then he gathered nearby manure into his trunk and threw it at the caretaker. By this act, the elephant clearly expressed his protest against his captivity. The elephant made it clear to everyone that he was cramped in his cell, there was no social life, and indeed he really wanted that mandarin.

This was the main thing: in the zoo no one wanted to understand: his only dream. After all, elephants also needed vitamins. But then the elephant's conversation with Alenushka was quickly interrupted. Barely dodging from the angry throw of the elephant, his caretaker tightly grabbed Alenushka arm and dragged her from the cage. And then all adults began scolding

her for the loss of the precious tangerine and dragged the kind girl away from the ZOO.

When they arrived home, only grandfather Fedor was

laughing at this adventure. Then he climbed onto the closet and gave Alenushka another hidden gift, which was intended to be given to Zinka's over-age son.

As it often happened before in the other places, tension was growing in the apartment of Fedor. Soon Grandma Anna quarreled with the brother's wife which happened during the New Year's Eve. Even to pronounce that they should eat rabbit was unpleasant to her. But the others, including Grandma, ate it and soon got very sick. After that event, saying in the apartment of the brother Fedor became completely intolerable, and they went back to Gelendzhik.

***

First Role

Children on the street where Alenushka spent most of her time did not often invite her to be part of their company. Moreover, their parents forbade visiting their homes, saying that she was illegitimate, and in general, a suspicious girl.

After learning such a strange thing, Alenushka stopped her efforts to join them for participation in the games. She did not want to humiliate herself asking anyone for anything. At the same time, Alenushka understood that she was more advanced than most the neighbor's children. She could run faster than many other children. She felt that she was more courageous than other children because she was not afraid of the animals walking on the street. Despite her very young age, she already had experienced life a lot and learned many different skills. Most importantly, she had traveled with her Grandma and met wolves. At the same time, most children and their parents never left the small town. All of the above gave her a feeling of superiority and somehow developed her leadership. In time, most small children respected her, considered her as the Queen of the street, seeking her friendship.

Once the older girls decided to create a street performance: "The Scarlet Flower". They painted invitations and let the younger children distribute them, advertise the play and invite their parents to come to watch it. Preparations were in full swing. But there was no special script, nobody learned the words or rehearsed it. One older girl just read the fairy tale out loud, and said that the "actors" will play whatever they remember, and one person would help them. That one person was called the "prompter". The prompter stayed behind the curtain, whispering the necessary words to those, who played the part. Then, the actors on the stage repeated their words in a loud voice.

One girl felt that she was the most important on the street. She wanted to play the main role in the play, but did not get it. So, at the last moment, she refused to play anything at all. On the other hand, Alenushka always dreamed to be with everyone and do things together, but not to be rejected all the time for some unclear reasons, as often happened before. She felt that it was an unprecedented happiness just to participate in the play. Therefore, she immediately agreed to replace that arrogant, snobby girl.

***

A magical improvised theater was arranged in the flower

 nursery. Bushes of evergreen shrubs formed the fabulous scenery there. The girls tied a blanket

to two trees, making it a "curtain for the stage." Before the performance, Alenushka felt proud and important. Her Grandma at heart was a real artist, had a wonderful voice, and in her youth was singing in the military club. Then, in Gelendzik, Grandma Anna went to the local choir that was at the Fishermen's Club. In any case, under the influence of Grandma's dream, Alenushka also secretly dreamed of a theater. The theater was for her like a bright temple of magic, where all dreams could come true.

Before the performance, Grandma took out her best dress from the old chest and put it on Alenushka. In order to create the effect of the old fashion, she put the sea life buoy under the dress. Thus, the long dress looked like a magnificent, nineteenth-century style dress. Then Grandmother rubbed the cheeks and lips of her granddaughter with beetroot for stage brightness.

Also, Alenushka asked to let her long hair fell down to the waistline like beautiful waves. With some admiration and joy, she whirled around and looked in the mirror.

"Well, you are the beauty!" - exclaimed the grandmother. *"I wish your mother could have seen you and be proud of you!"* But her mother would not be present.

In the flower nursery the rays of the setting sun painted everything in a mysterious appearance around the improvised stage. The audience sat right on the soft, fluffy carpet of warm grass anticipating the concert. Behind the curtain, a prompter clearly and slowly started to give everyone their clues. The play began.

Children completely forgot everything in the world, plunged into the magical world of the fairy tale, and played with great enthusiasm. From the bottom of their hearts, they believed in everything that was happening on the stage. It was real creativity, a tremendous revelry of improvisation.

The audience also watched with bated breath, keen on the play of their children. The mystic nature of the surroundings played its charming role. Finally, Alenushka came out to the stage to play her role, the "remorse of the elder sister" part. People exclaimed with surprise: - "Look, this is Alenushka!" This exclamation inspired the girl so much that she thought she was about to fly from joy and happiness.

Although there were no words in her part, she suddenly decided, to add them. So, she fell to her knees in front of her "younger sister" and shouted loudly: "*Forgive me for the sake of Christ! That was I, who hid your little scarlet flower*!" These words and actions were her personal findings, and the admiring spectators began to clap loudly. Probably, no real theater knew such energetic applause. Alenushka thought that everyone was amazed at her resourcefulness and artistry.

On this magical evening of universal delight, Alenushka thought that now she could only live under the applause of a loving audience. She dreamed of a theater where she could be free and do whatever would come to her mind. Then, for many years Alenushka lived in a beautiful world of this dream. Her most cherished desire burned inside and gave her beautiful meaning to all she did. This all-consuming dream about the real stage and theater was a protective shield and a sacred refuge from all her troubles.

***

Savior

Time was passing by. Alenushka continued to hide from the sad, poor reality in her own fantasies. The Russian folklore brought up her deep imagination and taught to love everything around. Living like a Cinderella, she still sometimes felt like a real star in her own world of her dreams. In the summer, at the most wonderful and beloved time of the year, some children went with their parents to a movie theater. They told wonders of the movie when they returned back. But nobody took Alenushka to the cinema. Grandpa never gave even the smallest amount of money for such "useless" entertainment. But Alenushka was not long upset for such trivialities. Most of the time she was left to herself and found pleasure in the simplest things. The girl with pleasure perceived nature around her as her own magical kingdom, loving everything she met there in the garden.

The small resort town Gelendzhik did not have a permanent theater. Even so, there were many talented people living in the town who participated in amateur performances. Also, in the summer, artists from the various touring theaters of other cities came to rest at the Black Sea and perform a little, making money, combining "business and pleasure." They were performing in sanatoriums, and in the open "Green Theater", or in the "Club of Fishermen".

Somehow one day Alenushka wandered into the resort

area and entered the Green Theater. There, the young children of the local "Youth Theater" performed "Cinderella". The play made a substantial impression on Alenushka. There was a real theater on the stage with real actors in real costumes. The emotional and enchanted girl stared at the stage, admiring the plot, loudly expressed everything that she thought about it. Suddenly, someone nearby, in an unexpectedly encouraging and sympathetic voice, said: - *"Come to us, to the "Youth Theater", dear. It's free. You can also take part in the plays and be on the stage."*

This elderly woman turned out to be the wife of the director of the Youth Theater. Participation in the theater was Alenushka's long-standing, biggest dream, her all-consuming passion. Therefore, the very next day she went to look for this mysterious Youth Theater, which was on the other side of the city in the "Pioneer House".

The Pioneer's House had a wonderful library and various educational free classes. It was very far from her home, but she tried to go there as often as she could. Once, someone at the library told Alenushka that the future actress should be developed in many areas. And she began to go to dancing classes, passed acting tests, and began to actively play in different performances.

The director of the Youth Theater and his wife were wonderful old people who gave their lives to children. During rehearsals they taught children how to move on the stage, and gave them the opportunity to play in the background. They suggested watching people and animals, copying and imitating them. When Alenushka acted in the background, she felt, that the audience carefully and with interest was watching her silent scenes. It gave her inspiration to play better.

After each performance, the strict director analyzed the acting of each actor. He said to Alenushka that with too much acting she "takes all attention to herself and it leads the viewer attention away from the main characters". He was teaching young actors to play together for one goal, to play as "an ensemble", and not to "pull a blanket over oneself for your own benefits and fame".

But his remarks and his teachings were not always taken in by the excited girl. Her passionate desire to be noticed was the most important reason why she started to go to the theater in the first place. She needed to get the love and admiration that she was deprived of in her home. And that was her main driving force, her motivation for everything she had ever done.

Each time appearing on the stage Alenushka continued to attract the attention of the audience with her expressive acting. Finally one day their director decided that it was time to give her the first lead role with the words. Alenushka was incredibly happy. She quickly learned her role, pondering it from all sides, creating her character. She practiced in the front of the mirror at home, working with gestures, turning her head, changing the sound of her voice, developing the movements, and improving her poses. She enjoyed this hard, but so wonderful and satisfying, job. She wanted to be the best in everything and everywhere. As she learned on the street, only the best people get all attention and rewards. So, it was her goal and she strived for it.

However, when she would come to the rehearsal, their director would find new options for the role, new shiny details. But he was also incredibly quick-tempered and often did not control himself. In a fit of anger, he threw chairs and broke something in the room. But Alenushka was not angry with him-

-her grandfather shouted even more. Therefore, she simply tried to follow the director's remarks and faithfully continued to attend her first theater school. At that Youth Theater, she spent her best school years.

Later Alenushka was living in her mother's newly built house. But there everything was commanded by the nasty stepfather her mother brought from Sakhalin Island. Alenushka felt even more sad, unhappy, and lonely there. Her "parents" were never interested in what she was passionate about, never came to her performances. They were occupied in their own life and were not participating in her life at all. She had no one to share her problems or her joy with.

Once the director announced that the theater will go on a two-week trip through the coastal cities of the Black Sea with the performances, like real artists. That was awesome news. Alenushka with incredible difficulty managed to convince her relatives to let her go on that trip. Having received permission, she simply "flew in the clouds."

The theater was the place where she was hiding from real life and all its problems, as she had done in early childhood in her grandmother's garden. It seemed to Alenushka that only on the stage she lived her real, full, emotional life. And in the Youth Theater, she spent several of the happiest years of her school life.

***

Binding Threads

In the summer of 1961, after several years of absence, mother Emma returned to Gelendzik with her new husband. They were building a new house near the Black Sea and planned to take Alenushka to live there. But Alenushka did not like her unpleasant, thin-lipped stepfather. Also, she did not want to leave her childhood place, where she was raised by her loving grandmother Anna. So, she tried to postpone that moment of separation.

Alenushka was standing near the low window, looking into the garden and listening to the radio. Suddenly the announcer indignantly broadcasted the shocking news. Twenty-year-old American student Victusha and his friend tried to hide a girl in the trunk of their car in order to transport her from East Berlin to West. But they were stopped, searched, and sent to prison. The boy's grandmother, Emma, like all his relatives, was terribly worried and tried to help him. Coincidentally, she had the same name as Alena's mother, which was a big surprise for the girl. At that time, while listening to Soviet radio hysterically condemning the American students, Alenushka could not imagine that in some magical way, thirty-five years later, this boy Victusha would become her devoted and loving husband. Then, her mother came to her and took her hand: "It is time to go to our new house!" But Alenushka loudly and firmly declared: "And I will live in America!"

In the 1960s, during the outbreak of the Cold War with America, to wish such a strange thing and in a loud voice was simply outrageous revolutionary blasphemy. So everyone just maliciously laughed at such an awkward, wild joke.

However, the invisible threads continued to weave the paths of fate and to connect the future with the present. The whirlwinds of fate, like the waves of a raging ocean, took off and fell, dragging a person along, and continuing to weave their connecting threads.

***

Road To Overcome

Once, Alenushka was reading a story named *"One who is walking will master any road"*. It made a great impression on her life. It was an inspiration and motivation, and in a difficult time, she always tried to remember it. This teaching story was describing:

Two people went to their cherished dream. Their path ran between steep mountain slopes with the danger threatened. Once they stopped in thought, for even from afar they saw that the road along which they walked ends at the nearest ledge. *"Ah, there is*

no further way! How stupid I was that I believed these dreams",
the first seeker thought. Doubt, fear, and unbelief confused him
and led him astray. He believed in his eyes instead of trusting
his heart and his dream. Turning around, he went back, never
reaching the cherished goal.

The second seeker at first hesitated too and stopped in
indecision. But unlike his fellow traveler, he believed his heart
and his dream. He doubted his vision. *"My dream cannot
be illusory, it cannot deceive the heart. I'm probably taking
something wrong,"* he thought. And then he decided to continue
the journey in the hope that a miracle would happen. Approaching
the bend, he exclaimed: *"Oh, Miracle!"*

But there was no miracle. Just approaching the ledge of
the rock, he saw that the road did not end at all, as it seemed
to him. The road further quietly turned behind a rock, beyond
which it was simply not visible. Turning around the turn, he saw
a small stretch of the path, the end of which was next to the cliff.
He reached the next dead end, and again a miracle happened.
And behind the slope appeared part of the path hiding behind it,
which ended at the ledge visible in front.

So he walked from one end of the path to the other, from the other to the third, from the third to the fourth. The farther the traveler went, the more the path opened for him. His heart had determination and self-confidence.

For the aspiring, nothing is impossible. For him, everything, even failure, and fall contribute to the ascent, becoming a step on the path to victory; because they help to see the error and correct it. And such people with renewed vigor, they again rise from knees to feet and go forward.

The first seeker returned home without passing his Path. He did not reach his cherished goal. Until now, he considers his dream to be unrealistic because he saw with his own eyes that there was no further way. He continued to live his former unsatisfied life.

And the second, stubborn, purposeful traveler himself became a conductor, who points the Way to all aspirants. And he taught not to be afraid of difficulties, failures, mistakes and falls. He taught that thanks to difficulties, a person becomes stronger, thanks to mistakes we can find the truth, and due to failures, we can become more enduring. The fact that for the former remained impossible, unbelievable, a pipe dream and a fairy tale has become a reality for the latter.

It is necessary to believe your heart. You must follow your dream, even if it seems unattainable and unrealistic. It is necessary to go forward if it seems that there is no further way. Maybe you, after taking a few steps, will see a miracle, and the next part of the path will open up to you, which until now seemed nonexistent. Remember, it depends on you what your dream will turn into - a pipe dream or reality!

***

Ask and you will be given.

I asked God for water, he gave me an ocean. I asked God for a flower, he gave me a garden. I asked God for a tree, he gave me a forest. I asked God for a friend, he gave me you. There is not enough darkness in the world to put out the light of one candle: The Candle of Love, Hope and Friendship. A candle loses nothing by lighting another candle".

***

On the Hill

Sixty years have passed. After many adventures, successful achievements, several marriages, after traveling the world during the "perestroika" Alenushka got a chance to leave Russia for good. "The winds of change" took her away to distant lands, to the kingdom of new life. She lived on the other continent of the Earth which was across the ocean.

She met the kind Knight Victusha in 1996, got married and moved to his citrus and avocado ranch soon after. She settled in his big house on the top of the hill where from the 1950th his family-owned about 3000 acres along the San Luis Rey River. The area around the house was surrounded by several dry hills and brown mountains. Since there were seldom rains in the area, the surrounding had dull colors all year round. The biggest, Lancaster Mountain, was very close to the house, and blocked the horizon view on the East. For many years that ranch house on the hill was a very quiet, spacious, and isolated place. Nothing was growing next to the house in the front yard.

On the West side of Victusha's property, below his hills, there was a "bedroom district" with several rows of houses stretching to the Highway. That small town was built around a lake, but soon that lake dried out, because lack of rain. After rare but prolonged heavy rains the San Luis Rey River usually flooded out of its banks and flooded both sides of the river. After such heavy rains, the inhabitants of the house were isolated in the house and observed only thousands of orchard trees around. But later the river dried out, as well, and many wild trees grew in its bottom.

The Ranch had its own wells, a very complex irrigation system, a cleaning system for drinking water and its own propane tank. Usually, the inhabitants of the house had a good supply of stored food for several locked-in days. When the dirt would dry a little, Victusha would get on his tractor and repaired the roads to the house to be able to get to the shopping or other places.

Soon after moving in the ranch, Alenushka began to plant cypress trees near the house, and made a special garden with fruit trees. But the ranch did not have any fence, and one day her cat and the dog were taken by the coyotes. Then Alenushka asked Victusha to put a fence around the house hill, and got two smart, courageous German Shepherd puppies. Alenushka was very happy with their devotion and love. Slowly the area down below their hill filled with houses, and the hum of the cars during peak hours on the Highway was reaching the house. That noise of civilization increased significantly over time and was especially strong around 6:00 am when Alenushka walked her dogs around their hills.

By the virtue of her energetic character and a vibrant personality, it was very difficult for Alenushka to live in such a quiet place. In Russia she was happy to have a very interesting and active life style, worked a lot, and moved all the time. Her grandmother used to say that while we are moving we are alive. But the quiet life on the Ranch was a strong contrast to her exciting life in St. Petersburg, and a great challenge. Alenushka very slowly became accustomed to the quiet and isolation of the place where she was living.

Since in the past Alenushka lived in a maritime climate, she was accustomed often enjoyed seeing the sea. When she came to live in the dry, dusty ranch, she tried to drive to the ocean as often as possible. The ocean was only about forty minutes of driving, and one day she persuaded her husband to buy a beach house. It was a wonderful resolution to all problems. However, since they lived far away in an isolated ranch on the hills, her every day communication was mostly with her dogs. The devoted dogs were very grateful and loving listeners.

Alenushka's creative mind was seeking a resolution. Soon, she established a dance school, and found some consolation in the dance teaching, organized charity events and performed in her productions. Then, her kind Victusha agreed to cruise around the world. However, it was still not very satisfying for energetic Alenushka, and she began to writer the books about her life in Russia and in America, about everything that she lived and observed.

Sixty years later, Alenushka was planting her garden far across the oceans. New garden was completely different and with a different soul. But still, it was very important to have own garden, and to share the blessing of it with all around. It was pleasant to please someone by giving fruits, flowers, berries or vegetables from it. Alenushka planted a fragrant garden to grow all kinds of healing herbs, as her kind grandmother taught her long time ago. Soon, she turned that garden hill into a fragrant paradise. All her old friends came back to her: the rabbits, honey bees, ants, and her dogs.

***

Beyond the Far Lands

One day, sixty years later, "The winds of Change" took her away from her mother land to a distant land, to the kingdom of new life. Alenushka lived on the top of the hill, on a ranch, among the mountains, citrus and avocado trees. At the ranch the most pleasant time for Alenushka was in the winter when the wind or the rain outside made a very cozy sound, and then it was good to be safe and comfortable at home. Alenushka felt some rest or some relaxation when there was rain.

The ranch had many different sounds that often at night could keep her awake. The irrigation system was working; the pump down below the hills in the orchard constantly made assuring noise, reminding that everything was fine on the ranch. After some rain, through the open windows Alenushka could hear the loud and happy chorus of frogs from the river, the grasshoppers, different insects and birds singing. At about midnight, the coyotes were yapping, and the dogs replied back to them. Victusha's grandfather's old clock was striking each hour, loudly reminding of the passing life. But the new clock upstairs that Alenushka gave her husband once was singing the music: *"Life is going on"*.

Every night, Alenushka was listening to that night music, thinking about what to do next, and how to live. She often missed all who lived one day far in her motherland but was gone forever. She often felt stressed but knew that she should just keep dancing, teaching, writing and traveling to feel happier. When she would go to the ocean was cleaning her energy and helped her to live in the strange land among strangers.

Once in a dream, the warm light came back to her from the

grandmother's yard and started shimmering with different colors, like in her childhood. When Alenushka woke up, she ran to her office and began to write her magical stories.

***

When Alenushka moved to California ranch one day, she began to plant her own fragrant garden, pick up all kinds of healing herbs, as her kind fairy, her grandmother Anna taught her long time ago. Soon, she turned her garden hill into a fragrant paradise. All her old friends came back to her: the rabbits, honey bees, ants, dogs.

Once, in the memory of her childhood adventure in Gelendzik with her grandfather, Alenushka planted a bush of blackberries. She planted it near the metal fence, which enclosed a huge hill near the house. But while planting this bush of blackberries, Alenushka completely forgot about the huge energy of this generous and mysterious plant. The uncontrollable passion and love for the life of blackberries knew no barriers or prohibitions.

The blackberry began to violently break through the metal mesh of the fence, without asking anyone for permission. First, the bush threw their branches far ahead. Then, it was reaching the ground and immediately grabbed onto it and sprouted deep. A year later, a blackberry filled the entire fence, stretching far in all directions. In April many small white flowers appeared on the bushes. Then, many berries quickly jumped out and quickly ripened. Alenushka daily collected a whole bucket of berries, competing with birds. But the generous bush gave her new berries already blushing on the bushes. And the ripe berries were getting dark, tasty, and nutritious. Another blackberry was playing with Alenushka, hiding under the many leaves, trying to stay longer in their own native home.

Once, while collecting blackberries, Alenushka opened the well of her memory. It began to spin like a kaleidoscope of her past events, and she glimpsed back at many adventures of her childhood.

"Ah, these black eyes, they captivated me," – her dear grandmother Anna sang again quietly and somehow very thoughtfully. Without stopping the song, she cautiously looked at her severe husband Minai, a former retired major. She was afraid of his harshness, afraid that he would hear her song, would shout that she must be silent. Anna loved and knew many songs of the dissident Peter Leshchenko, banned in the USSR. His songs were full of longing for Russia.

Although the 1950's were already called the "Khrushchev Thaw", and there were no strangers in the house, the old fear of Stalinist terror lived nearby. This deep slavish fear made one look back in any conversation, and look around, and to speak in a whisper. But Grandmother Anna, despite her husband's prohibitions, taught her granddaughter Alenushka the lyric songs of the exile Petr Leshchenko. His songs sounded in the

Alenushka memory, reminding her beautiful blond mother, who so rarely visited her daughter, and about her loving grandmother, who was taking care of the girl with such deep love. Petr Leshchenko sang: *"I'm not walking in my mother-land. But a gloomy morning wakes up. Do you remember me, my dear, golden-haired woman?"*

The blackberry sang this song with Alenushka to the immortal voice of the beautiful singer Petro Leshchenko. *"I miss my homeland, the Russian fields, the green noise of foliage, and the gray beloved eyes."*

Alenushka mother Emma, Grandmother Anna, severe grandfather Minai, and all other relatives long ago went into the other world, melted in the fog of eternity. But the memory of them lived inside Alenushka soul, and they all were alive. It was

especially good to talk with the good fairy, her beloved grandmother Anna whom Alenushka often asked for wise advice. And Grandmother always told her that the goodness conquers evil. For a long time Alenushka walked towards this ancient wisdom until she grasped the depth of its meaning.

Here, in the California garden while listening to Alenushka songs, the honey bees stopped buzzing and the rabbits stopped running. Her devoted dogs attentively were looking at their mistress, ready to serve and comfort her, giving boundless, unconditional and faithful love.

The cheerful Alenushka did not want to give up or lose her heart. She remembered that long time ago the blackberries near the Dolmen were teaching her something important. Now she knew that: with a dream and love in the heart, any person can build a very strong house anywhere on Earth. Dreams and love give strength to overcome any obstacles.

***

Love

Two German Shepherds Tuzik and Sonia lived in the garden and enjoyed playing there when Alenushka went out to be there with them. Then, her dogs attentively were looking at their mistress with their clever brown eyes always ready to love, serve, and comfort her. The dogs were very intelligent and knew many words. They were listening carefully to their owner and watched all people around. They knew in advance what the owners wanted from them, and tried to do it to make them happy.

Around the front yard, there was a special fence that the dogs would not run away to the fruit orchards. Also, that fenced territory included a big hillside garden with different fruit trees, flowers, and bushes. But the dogs were accustomed to do their private toilet business outside of it. Alenushka was happy about the dog's habit to keep the garden near the house clean. So, this is why several times a day, she took her dogs for a walk on the different ranch roads.

Dog Sonia was very sociable and did not want to play alone. She was sure that her friend must be Tuzik. But Tuzik was very jealous that younger dog Sonia took all attention of his owners. But since the owners loved her, Tuzik decided to be tolerant of her, as well, and slowly became accustomed to the cheerful and playful Sonia.

Sona generally thought that her existence was to make everybody happy. This is why she waved her tail, and kisses everybody. That was her nature. Alenushka prohibited dogs to jump on her with kisses and hugs. Then, Sonia learned that a nice man Victusha did not tell her anything about it. So every time Sonia saw Victusha she jumped very high and kissed him.

It was her way of saying; *"I love you the most because you never scold us for anything."* Since no strangers would come near the house, the dogs were bored without barking and protecting something. They wanted to do their job guarding the property of the owners. But often there was nobody to protect from. From time to time, they were very happy when they could exercise their rights to work and fulfill their duty to protect the property from all kinds of intruders. The happy time for the German shepherds was the time when the postman or delivery man would drive

up to the house, or the pickers would come to get the avocados and oranges. Then, the dogs barked with all their strength, excited about the opportunity to show off their skills. After such a well-done job, they always wanted to go out and to mark all the territory around. Then, they would come back home with the desire to eat something delicious.

Tuzik and Sonia wanted to hunt neither rabbit nor squirrels. First, it was too hot during the day to hunt. Tuzik was already pretty old and did not want to move much without a very good reason. The dogs were waiting for Alenushka to walk them and tell them what they should do. So most of the days they just were lying down on the steps of their stairway or on the patio and did not want even to move their ears.

On hot days they enjoyed swimming in the swimming pool, retrieving their toys. This is why Alenushka bought for each of them their own pool, and dogs jumped in it to cool off. Also, Alenushka put two treadmill machines in the garage, and from day one, she trained her dogs to exercise on the treadmill. Dogs knew that they had to jump onto it and run for several minutes before getting their dinner. Sometimes, the young dog Sonia did not want to do such (useless, as she was thinking) movements. So, when nobody saw her, she would jump off the machine and hide behind running Tuzik. So Alenushka started to tie her up to the bar of the machine, and Sonia learned not to go away without permission. They enjoyed the exercise in the garage only on rare cool days and only because they wanted to please their owners.

***

Circle of Eternity

One day the dogs came out to play when it was getting dark. Suddenly they got very excited, started to jump to the trunk of the Palm tree. Alenushka came closer, and in the thickening darkness she saw an unusual animal, hanging upside down, barely clinging to a tree trunk. She called her husband, who came quite quickly, brought the flashlight, and immediately recognized in this strange animal a baby owl!

A small, fluffy owl, all still covered with children's down, was stuck on the trunk of a palm tree. Alenushka locked her dogs in the yard and tried to find a long and convenient tool to help the owl. Then she went into the house and brought a soft, fluffy dust brush on a long stick, which the housekeeper used to collect the cobwebs under the high ceilings. Then, Victusha handed it to the baby owl. The owl immediately grabbed this fluffy brush, and again hung upside down on it. Alenushka was concerned for this huge but helpless chick, and suggested to put the owl in the back of the truck.

The night was fast falling and soon the coyotes would come to get the helpless baby owl. Coyotes were getting more and bold, and often came to the fence near the house, where the dogs were angrily barking at them. On such nights Alenushka was not be able to sleep and would walk out with a gun to shoot and to scare the coyotes away. From the loud sound the gun, they ran away further, but then they would come back, looking for some food at the trash cans. If at such night Alenushka would release her brave dog Tuzik, courageous African shepherd would rush after the coyotes, regardless of their numbers. But he was already old and his legs were failing, betraying him. But his strength of mind was still the same young.

And another dog, the little German shepherd Sonya was very cute and looked just like a ballerina. She was bypassing the puddles from afar and stepped cautiously, afraid to get dirty. She believed that her main role was just to express a lot of love for her owners, to kiss them or just wave the tail to all who were paying attention to her. Once the old Tuzik said that he is tired of teaching her to bark and protect the property. And she often answered that it was his specific purpose and job to do. So, Victusha carried the baby Owl to his truck for safety, and the little owl laid down there without strength. His mother was very upset, flew close by, called and asked her baby owl to try to take off again. The baby Owl just was lying down on his back and breathed heavily with fear and helplessness. He was such a nice puffy little ball. But when Alenushka came closer to him with the water, he spread his wings and bounced off. He had good and strong wings, but he simply did not know what to do with them. It was his first night, when he was just learning how to fly. Then, Alenushka went to the backyard to get some dog's dry food for the bird. But when she returned, the baby owl was already gone. *"So he was able to take off!"* - They rejoiced.

Remembering his helplessness, Alenushka was afraid that he did not have enough strength to fly up a tree. So, she asked Victusha to walk around with a flash light, looking for the little owl. They found him sitting quietly on the edge of the road. The little baby owl was looking at the people with his large, innocent eyes, and his mother's voice was heard nearby. In the warm April night the mother Owl continued teaching her chick to fly. Victusha said: "*Let nature go its own way.*"

Happiness and peace reigned in the night. How long such serene happiness would reign, how much time the happy family have on the ranch with no troubles from the wildness.

***

On the next night during the evening walk, Alenushka and Victusha were happy to hear how the Owl father taught his cub to hoot as all Owls should to do. The owl mother was sitting a little further from the baby, letting the father have the opportunity to express his love for their cub. Only occasionally she sent them her approval and her enthusiasm for the new successes of her son. The father Owl was doing it first loudly and confidently. Then, he asked his baby to repeat it after him. But the cub just mumbled back something silly by his thin and tender voice. Their voices were clearly audible in the night. Nearby, a happy young mother Owl also taught something to the chick. Then, the owl father was teaching his son also hunting lessons. The father-owl brought a mouse to the nestling, and the baby-owl was still enjoying a free breakfast in the parent's house.

The parents-owls were so much involved in the teaching their son that they did not notice that the night is over. The safe, comfortable dark night was their friend, but it was already gone. With the rising sun, the danger of daylight came for the owls. Alenushka and her dogs headed towards the house, reassured that the baby-owl continues to comprehend the basics of hard life at the ranch.

Suddenly, from the side of the last palm tree, where there was a hawk's nest, a terrifying, warlike cry started. Alenushka

looked up. A huge hawk was rushing to the place where the father-owl was sitting with the chick. Alenushka tried to scare away that hawk, but he did not pay any attention to her waving hands and tiny yells. At the same time, but a little further, she heard a warning, excited cry of an owl-mother. But it was too late. The Owl father tried to protect his little baby as courageously as he could and covered his son with his body. But what could an owl do against a huge hawk?

The next night, walking before bedtime with dogs, no one heard the happy scream of an owl, the babbling of its new cubs, or the hoot of their father - owl. Over the ranch was an oppressive, deathly silence.

Three days later, the owl mother began to search for her husband. She flew from one tree to another tree, visiting the places where they spent their happy time with her husband-owl. She called him very loudly, with desperation, in a dreary voice. Then, in the next night, she flew onto the roof of the house, where they on the moon light nights so often happily were meeting before. She screamed for a long time, with longing and despair. But no one responded to her call.

Alenushka could not sleep. She understood well the language of animals. And while for a long time living on a ranch, she learned to understand the language of birds. Finally, she got up, walked outside, and said to the owl: *"If you find yourself a friend, fly in and settle closer to the house. And I will try to protect you from the hawks. "*

After this incident, Alenushka walked everywhere with her gun, trying to scare away the Hawks and get revenge for the gentle owls. For the next three days, Mother Owl was silent. Then for several days she flew from tree to tree, sat next to the house, calling for her friend. And suddenly, a Miracle happened, and her Friend flew to her. Life went on. Life was in a circle of eternity...

***

Hawk

While living on the ranch, Alenushka observed that every animal brought its own benefit to nature or was serving for something. One was a predator and hunted for someone. The other was someone's prey. It was a natural circle of life.

There were many tall palms trees along the western road. Victusha planted them many years ago to protect his avocado trees from the strong setting sun. At the end of this road there was a hawk's nest high on the last tree. There were many of them breeding in the recent years on the comfortable ranch. Victusha was happy of that, because they eat the rats, squirrels and other small animals. But Alenushka did not like these strong predators. Especially one of them bothered her all the time. He loudly and heavily shouted during the hunt, disturbing her soul. The hawks had more bold personality than the crows. Hawks flew very close to the house, ravaged the nests of songbirds, and ate the chicks. They were not afraid of either shots or screams.

The crows were one of the smartest and the most loathed vultures on the ranch. Alenushka often saw how these greedy robbers, treacherous crows devastate someone's nests and destroy someone's lives. She always tried to scare them away from the house trees, where singing birds made their nests. Sometimes she shot at them with her gun, but never hit any of them.

One spring, Alenushka and her dogs Tuzik and Sonya were walking on their hill and came to the last palm trees, which were far from home. From a distance they already saw that the crows flew in a huge flock to the high palm tree, where the Hawk's nest was. They made horrific and greedy noise of hunting, and worked as a team. Several crows were sitting on the palm tree and watching if the Hawk was coming down to protect his chicks.

And at the same time the others were pecking everything that was in the nest. Then they changed their roles. At that moment, the hawk-parent was hunting somewhere, looking for food for its chicks. His babies were helpless in the absence of their parents.

While seeing such a cruel event, Alenushka did not want that the crows would take advantage of the unprotected chicks in the Hawk's nest. She and her loyal dogs ran to the palm tree together, shouting and waving their arms, trying to scare off the crows. But it was too late. When the Hawk arrived, there was nothing in the nest. The Hawk sat on a branch near the destroyed nest, holding food in its beak. He turned his head looking for the enemies, but the crows were far gone.

After this incident, the Hawk settled higher on a nearby mountain among the neighbor's avocado plantations. He was no longer young, and very smart and observant. Soon he realized that on the palm trees near the house various songbirds were building nests and raising tasty chicks. Especially gullible pigeons were very easy prey for the fast Hawk.

The pigeons lived in pairs. Most of the day, they hid under the shady trees of the garden. But sometimes they flew out into the open area or sat on the wide road leading to the house picking up seeds. They took off only at the last moment when a car or a dog was rushing very close towards them. Occasionally they sat on the fence, looking around with curiosity and gently, quietly cooing. Sometimes at such moment the swift hawk dived down headlong, with a wild cry, and bit off the stupid pigeon's head. Then, at the same great speed, he immediately, in a hurry, flew back.

One day, the observant Hawk noticed that local Owls nested on the western side of the hill near Alenushka house. But only at sunrise and sunset did the Owls fly out of their hiding place to hunt or teach their children. At that time, the smart and always hungry Hawk also often would come to the western side of the hill. He would circle there, waiting for the Owl or its cubs to appear.

One evening Alenushka, Victusha and their dogs Tuzik and Sonya walked along the western road near the palm trees. Suddenly they saw the Hawk circling high in the sky. Hawk was huge, and easily could grab a rabbit, a duck or a cat and take it away to his nest. Only snakes were often daring to get away from the Hawk.

Alenushka saw the Hawk and immediately began to run excitedly back and forth, waving her jacket and shouting loudly at the Hawk. The dogs became agitated as well, began to jump, and even tried to take off. Seeing such noise down below, the Hawk obviously was estimating if he was strong enough to get one of the dogs for his meal. But the German Shepherds were too big for the Hawk.

At the same time he was very surprised at such annoying noise and an unexpected hindrance to his hunt. Then, he began to circle lower and lower, descending closer and closer to Alenushka and her dogs. The Hawk went down so low that Alenushka saw his sharp eyes, all-seeing at long distances. The King of the ranch was clearly surprised that anyone at all had the courage to shout something angrily at him or to indicate how and where he should hunt. There were no such daredevils in nature who would threaten the hawk's control or freedom.

The King of the Sky examined everyone below him on the ground and laughed venomously. It was clear to him that nothing threatened his hunt. But the sun had already set below the horizon and painted the west in bright colors. The Hawk flapped his wings and flew off to the distant mountain to his new home. Apparently he decided that it was better not to risk it and stay away from such loud dogs, and people waving their arms and jackets. After that and for a long time, Alenushka did not see this Hawk on the western side of the ranch.

***

The Little Mouse

One summer it was incredibly hot in the front yard. On such unpleasant days, the German Shepherd Tuzik hid in the cool garage. And another dog Sonia stayed on the grass in the shade of the cypress trees. Also, it was relatively cool under the umbrellas which stood by the porch. Alenushka put there two huge lounges for the dogs and the lounges served them as resting places. Some other living creatures of the courtyard tried also to stay in the shade of the umbrellas. When sometimes the door would be open for a minute, the wonderful coolness of the house poured out onto the hot tiles of the sunny yard.

Once upon a time, a small and inexperienced mouse, seeing that there were no dogs nearby, came up to the porch, trying to hide from the heat. When the house door opened, the mouse with no hesitation rushed into the saving coolness of the house.

Suddenly, finding himself in an unknown corridor, the frightened and stunned Little Mouse immediately hid under a table. For some time he sat there quietly, trying to understand where he was and how dangerous it was for him. However, after a while the Little Mouse felt severe hunger. He began to run around the huge house looking everywhere for some food. But the floor in the house was often washed, observing perfect cleanliness, and there were practically not even small crumbs anywhere.

Having run around the whole house, Little Mouse visited its highest floor and the lowest floor but did not find anything edible. Several times he came across the owners of the house, but immediately slipped under the stove in the kitchen. The owners were surprised to see the unusual and strange presence of a scurrying Little Mouse inside the house, who so openly ran around their house in broad daylight, without fear of anything. The hostess even exclaimed:

"Look, the little mouse is running around here like he is in a park! And he did not fall into the mousetrap! So, I'll put out a lure, peanut butter on a sticky trap." And she left to set tempting mouse traps.

The hungry Little Mouse received a huge dose of mortal fear from meeting the owners, and hid under the other table in the corridor. Slowly, it became clear to him that running around someone else's house all day long was incredibly dangerous. He felt that even if he is a very hungry little boy, it still would be better to look for some food at night. But most importantly, he grimly realized that in the house there was no safe shelter for him and no exit to the freedom of the yard.

However, the Little Mouse loved his past life outside, and he wanted, by all means, to find a way to salvation, a way to freedom. At night the Little Mouse again tried his luck in search of food and a hole to the outside. Suddenly, once again running along the corridor, he smelled the pleasant smell of an incredibly tasty delicacy. The Little Mouse cautiously approached this seductive scent, which was located in the middle of a wide plate. But the odor of danger also came from this strange sheet. This second dangerous smell surrounded the wonderful food in the middle of the plate. For Little Mouse, a terrible dilemma emerged: what to do, and how to get that delicious food. What will prevail in the Mouse: the feeling of hunger or the feeling of fear?

Tired Little Mouse could not fight his hunger anymore. However, he was extremely smart and remembered the stories his grandmother Big Mouse told him about the danger of the delicious and free food on the unknown plate. Also, The Little Mouse was also very talented and he calculated the distance correctly. He understood that in order to get to the edge of the food, he needed to jump as hard as he could. So, he did it.

He luckily landed not in the dangerous middle of that trap. Indeed, he got very close to the delicious Peanut Butter left by the hostess for him in the sticky mousetrap. The Little Mouse quickly ate this delicacy, and immediately felt much better. Then, he looked around and remembered that his wise grandmother Big Mouse had taught him not to trust either the delicious smell or the sweetest food in an unfamiliar house.

The Little Mouse realized that it was time to escape from this incredibly pleasant paradise. But still, his paws were slightly glued to the mouse trap-sticky. First, the Little Mouse thought that "the morning is wiser of the evening," and he might stay overnight in this place. But then the words of his wise grandmother Big Mouse sounded:

"If you ever would get into a people's house, do not eat or drink anything for three days. Try to get out of there, no matter what. But if you tempted and tasted something incredibly delicious on the "sticky" place, try to lick it out from your paws and jump out of it. "

At night, the hostess heard the fuss of the Little Mouse on the mousetrap and came to him. The Little Mouse suddenly saw a huge scary Hostess. But the Little Mouse realized that this person was his only salvation, and could help him to escape. Then, the Little Mouse took all his courage as the last chance for freedom, and shouted with all his might: *"Help, Save! Don't let me die here! "*

His eyes were sparkling begging for help. For most Men, such a creature is just a dirty mouse that spreads infection everywhere. But for the hostess of this house the Mouse's plea did not go unnoticed. His thin voice sounded despaired, and

174

the hostess took the mousetrap outside, and put the bait with the mouse on a high post. The Little Mouse was delighted with the fresh air. He knew that only freedom and happiness smelled like that. But how he could break away from the terrible glue?

The Little Mouse looked around and realized that only one place on the mousetrap was not so sticky. This place still had traces of Peanut Butter. Although the mouse was very small, he was still very smart. He also loved advice of his wise grandmother - Big Mouse. He started to lick his front legs for a long time, trying to clear them of the terrible glue. Then he stretched out and put his clean paws in the place of Peanut Butter, where the glue did not work and did not hold the Little Mouse. Then, suddenly, the Little Mouse heard nearby the real voice of his loving grandmother. The Big Mouse came very close to the Little Mouse and pulled him out of the mousetrap.

From the moment when the Little Mouse disappeared in the house, his many relatives searched for him all night and almost despaired of seeing him alive. Suddenly they smelled the Little Mouse nearby and ran to his aid. So his grandmother - the Big Mouse - came to his rescue first. She scrambled onto the pole and began to help the little Mouse get rid of the glue.

The other worried relatives were trying to help the little Mouse, also. So his effort became much stronger. The love and support of his family gave more confidence and strength to exhausted and scared Little Mouse. He pulled himself up, caught on the clean edge of the glue, and pulled away from the place that held him so tightly. Then, feeling the long-awaited freedom, the Little Mouse with great relief started to run away from the horrible mousetrap. And all his relatives ran with him. They went to celebrate the miraculous release of the Little Mouse.

In the morning the Hostess came to see what happened to the mousetrap. But there was nothing on the mousetrap. This is how the smart and talented Little Mouse escaped the deadly trap. The love and care of his family who were looking for him all night also helped him to stay alive.

***

Rattlesnakes

The area around the hills and the house was full of poisonous rattlesnakes. Usually, they started to move well in southern California from May and until October when it was hot. During the winter, they were still hiding there everywhere, as well, but they did not like the cold weather and didn't move much during the cool season.

Several times Alenushka saw the rattlesnakes when she walked her dogs along the ranch roads. When the dogs were very young they were taken to a special school, where they were taught to avoid the snakes. However, once at night, Tuzik did not see the snake in advance and was bitten. He yelled from the terrible pain, his leg got swollen very fast, but while strongly limping he came back home begging for help. Alenushka knew

that vitamin K is good against poison and gave him two pills of it right away. Then, she took her dog to the hospital, where the veterinarian doctor tried to save his life for the whole night. After that tragic event, the nerves in the leg of the dog were damaged. Tuzik barely could handle the heat, and could not stop on the hot ground.

Another time, during the evening before the sunset Alenushka walked with her dogs along the road near the persimmon orchard. She always was holding her younger and highly emotional dog Sonia on the leash. But old Tuzik, as always, was freely running ahead of them. Suddenly, he stood silently and stretched his head towards the rattlesnake. The snake was about two meters in front of him. Alenushka and Sonia also stopped and waited. They saw the terrible, poisonous rattlesnake was tightly folded into a tense coil, ready to attack. She apparently hunted for squirrels and was ready to straighten her rings in a huge leap toward her victim.

When the snake felt that Tuzik came too close to her, she began to rattle her tail with a terrifying sound that made everyone feel cold in the blood. Alenushka thought: *"Well, we were lucky this time! This snake at least warned us in advance!"*

The snake hissed: *"I am your death! Do not come any closer!"* And they went around her a long distance. But a minute later they heard from afar the terrible dying scream of a bitten squirrel. The snake got its dinner.

Another hot summer night a rattlesnake was chasing the mice and crept up to the house porch. It made a lot of menacing, threatening noise, ready to bite and kill anybody by her poison.

178

The dog Tuzik was barking at her trying to get the snake away from the house. But the snake felt it was trapped and raised her upper body ready to strike. Courageous Knight Victusha came out with a gun, shot the snake, and then he took a shovel and threw it from the hill. Fortunately, this time the evil plans of the snake did not work out for her. Alenushka washed the porch with chlorine, thinking: "To keep the family safe, to cherish the loved ones, everybody always should be watching for the warning signs and be very careful."

The ranch life continued to write its book by moving her hand, putting everything that was happening around on the paper. The ranch was teaching: *"Do not trust even a smiling snake"*.

***

Singing Birds

Many colorful birds lived on the Ranch. Early in the morning they especially enjoyed being in the garden where they found many constantly blooming flowers. Also, they were around the swimming pool area, close to the house, where it was safer. In March singing birds began to look for the partners with whom they could play their love games. March was a very noisy and busy time for the birds, especially very early in the mornings. They mostly were singing beautiful songs of love and glorifying joyful life. Alenushka put several birds' houses in the garden and they occupied them right away. It was pleasant to wake up to the birds' songs.

Then in April the birds finally formed their families and began making their nests. However, the birds learned that their nests could be broken by crows and hawks. So they got smarter, trying to build their nests in more protected locations, and were building their nests in the low part of the cypress or palm trees, mostly inside the front yard.

In May the singing birds began to lay eggs in the nests getting loudly yelling babies. When Alenushka would be feeding her dogs, the little baby birds also would be yelling very loudly because they are always hungry. However, there were a lot of bold nasty crows on the ranch, who busted songbird nests. In the early morning, the crows were coming very closer to the house, sitting on the palm trees, watching the birds. Other crows were coming silently at sunset, cruising around the palm trees, and looking for the nests. Also, in their cowardly and insolent nature, the crows were accustomed to act out of the blue, out of cunning and meanness. For example, when the mother of a singing bird flew for food for her chicks, the crows flew to the unprotected nests and attacked the tender chicks.

It is amazing that in the spring when singing birds fed their chicks, some other members of their family worked as guards. They were sitting high on the trees looking out for the enemies. They were incredibly courageous, these little birds. And with all their bravery, they were guarding their nests. Without hesitation,  without fear, they ran at any size of the enemy and rushed into the battle for the protection of their offspring. Alenushka often saw a very small bird fearlessly pursuing a crow or hawk many times bigger than the singing bird. Sometimes, two little birds were chasing their enemies trying to peck them. But still, they needed people to help them.

The German Shepherds Tuzik and Sona were learning

from their mistress, or possibly out of the boredom and inactivity, became used to reacting to the crows, as well. Tuzik periodically was expressing his concern about birds invading his property. He was barking at them, urging the hostess to act immediately: "*It is the time to do something drastically against these aggressive birds.*"

If Alenushka heard them, she jumped out of the house to shoot at the yelling bandit crows. Even though she never hit one crow, they were afraid to even of her loud screams and her waved arms. Seeing the dogs and Alenushka with a gun, the crows were loudly yelling in nasty hoarse voices and flew away so fast, that even their feathers were raining down.

***

Feed Yourself

The birds have different voices for different events, and all of them sing loudly and talk to each other activities throughout the day. One day Alenushka was watching a bird family with a new son Bobby. Every early morning and before the sunset, they came to get some food nearby the front door on the meadow. Mother Bird always walked first, far from her husband and far from her adorable, but a little noisy, son. She liked to enjoy her breakfast alone, in peace and solitude. Her husband was not as lucky as she, and could not have one peaceful meal. Their son is always hungry, and it looked like the father had to feed him.

The bird Bobby was almost the same size as his parents, but he did not want to do anything for himself. He was running at his father's side, with wide-open mouth, and with a very loud cry: *"Give me more, give more - give more!"*

When he sees that his father got something from the under the grass, Bobby immediately pushed his open mouth to his father. It looked like his father did not have any choice, but to give him what he found. The baby bird Bobby was trying to run as close as possible to his father and yelled almost without stopping. The squeaky, loud voice of a lazy son, his persistently open mouth, his annoying begs for more food was unbearable for his parents. Several different birds came and looked at this annoying scene, but disapproved of it, and escaped on their own business.

It looked like the hard-working father did not have any time to eat for himself. He made a strong effort in teaching his son how to get food on his own. He had shown it to Bobby several times and told him to try to do it independently. The baby bird picked a couple of times the ground randomly without real searching it, did not find anything, and gave up. He saw that it was much easier to acquire the food from the work of his father, and continued running after his father with his widely opened mouth, loudly yelling: *"more food, give me more food!"*

Every day Alenushka could recognize the distinguished voice of the Baby Bird. But in several days, the father changed his techniques. When he saw some food down in the grass, he would stop near it, waiting when his son would come closer. Then, the smart father ate what he found and run away from his hungry and unskilled son. But Bobby kept running after the father, demanding the food, instead of looking down and finding the seeds in the grass. His mother came close to them and watched for a while what they were doing. But soon she was annoyed by the yelling and the demanding voice of the baby bird so much, that she quickly jumped between the baby and his father and pushed the boy away. The baby bird was shocked by that action of his mother, stood for a moment with no yelling.

On the next day, the father bird tried something new. He would find some good food in the grass and take it in his mouth. But instead of giving the food to his Baby Bird, his father was just holding the delicious snack in his own mouth, looking in a different direction. His son first did not know what to do, but as always, he looked up and opened his mouth. But his father did not give Bobby that desirable snack. Instead, he swallowed it himself. After that his father began to run away, yelling back: *"Try again, my son. All food is under your feet, just look for it!"* The bird Bobby had no choice but to find some food by himself. On the next morning after breakfast, the baby bird and his parents had a family meeting. With joy and excitement, they stated, that their son had gained the skills of food finding. Now it was a different agenda, and his parents discussed it simultaneously with big excitement. It was time to teach him some social skills. The baby bird with a cheerful initiation asked his parents: *"Should I learn how to fit well in the bird community?"*

The parents stopped talking for a while from this unexpectedly mature statement from their son. Then Father said: *"God gave you parents. But you will make your own friends with your own choice. When you will get them, try to keep them for a lifetime.*" And his mother continued: "*We are happy only when we have someone to share our happy time with. The more you share the more joy you will feel, and the happier you will be.*" With these wise thoughts, they let Bobby alone.

The next morning, the bird family was again on the meadow, and the baby bird was respectfully walking between his proud parents, finding food on his own. When his effort was successful, he was very excited, but still tried to talk to his parents very politely. And they cheerfully, with attention, answered him. It was obvious that Bobby had learned a very important lesson. He learned that in order to succeed in the bird's society, it is very important to be pleasant to everybody around. On the closest tree, Alenushka saw one family of birds who were singing their glory to the new and beautiful day. She watched them for a while, and then went on her own human life.

***

Defeat Fears

Fear, although still small, began to live inside Alenushka when she was a smal child, and often tormented the girl for various reasons, preventing her from sleeping. The little girl did not know how to deal with Fear. And over time, Fear invited his Friends, other little Fears. They circled around the Girl and disturbed her Soul, preventing her from living joyfully and freely. But once a wise Fairy, a loving grandmother Anna, said to Alenushka: "Fear happens to all Living Beings, both the smallest and the very large. But every creature reacts differently to Fear. It depends on how the Living Being responds to Fear, whether he wins or dies. For example, different animals live in the forest, both large and small. And even bears are afraid of something. They are afraid of the brave Wolverine, who even attacks the wolves and takes their prey. In addition, Wolverine is very hot-tempered and it is able to fight even with a bear, driving it onto a tree!

Even in loose snow, the wolverine can jump and not fail. And the heavy bear will immediately bog down. Bears generally do not really like to spend their calories, so it's better to bypass the wolverine

Even in the Jungle there are huge animals that are afraid of something," continued the grandmother. "For example, elephants are not afraid of mice. But they suffer from very small but deadly snakes that can, if not kill, then cripple, if not an adult elephant, then their cubs. Therefore, when they see a snake in the distance, elephants immediately change their direction of movement.

Kind grandmother Anna told her granddaughter: *"And you, Alenushka, do not be afraid of Fear. Fear is strong only as long as you are afraid of something. When you stop being afraid, Fear will run away from you. Never let your fear decides your future."* Alenushka was very surprised at such a simple solution. She had long wanted to defeat Fear.

One day, Fear weakened and fled. Every time the girl overcame Fear, she was getting stronger and stronger. The Soul grew resilient and tougher. Finally, Alenushka grew up a fearless lady. She was not afraid of anything, and Fear was increasingly defeated. Fear ran away from her - far, far away. So she was able to succeed in all her endeavors. And she became an outstanding Person who conquered all Fears.

***

Alenushka always remembered the lessons of her grandmother, who told her: *"To be a strong person, you have to learn to have every day a winning attitude. It is important to keep motivations, visualize what you want to achieve, and strive for it."* Even in her youth, thinking about her adventures, Alenushka realized that reality often turns out to be completely different from what it seems at first glance. But then, in the bustle of life, she did not have free time to describe in detail her unusual incidents or experiences. In Russia, she always had a very eventful life with constant novels, hobbies, and travels, struggles and emotions. There was not a day left to stop, look back, and think. But most importantly, she was afraid to look into the painful depths of her memory, to look back at the tragedies of the past. It was painful for her to return at a time when not far from the Lermontov monument, in the area of the current "Arch of Love", her future parents met on the dance floor.

All her life, Alenushka built sandcastles, dreamed, and believed in miracles. The fragile castles crumbled, and she began to build new ones, even under the threat of a huge wave that was about to wash away everything she had created. But she never gave up. The main thing was the process that pleased her and helped her through difficulties.

One day, the time came when she escaped from captivity and she did not need to fight for survival. She lived in calm transatlantic silence, far from all sorts of troubles, and took her little dogs for a walk around citrus plantations on a hill. And sometimes, she shot jackals, rattlesnakes, and scared the raven with the help of her gun. She even had her own dance school. She taught students how to comprehend the life of dance.

Alenushka always believed that miracles live nearby; they just need to be seen. Miracles will become more vibrant and clearer if each event is perceived from the positive side, and try to see the light and joy in everything.

The main thing in the life of any person is to cultivate, cherish, and keep in his soul love for at least something. This inner feeling of love will help overcome many difficulties. We must love life with all our might because it is so beautiful. This inner love is the main meaning of life.

Copy Rights

Author is Elena Pankey. All rights reserved. No part of this publication may be reproduced, distributed, or transmitted in any form or by any means, including photocopying, recording, or other electronic or mechanical methods, without the prior written permission of the publisher, except in the case of brief quotations embodied in critical reviews and certain other noncommercial uses permitted by copyright law. The title of a book printed in the United States of America. The main category of the book is Biography, memorial. Other category is Family, Soviet Union. First Edition was in 2020.

***

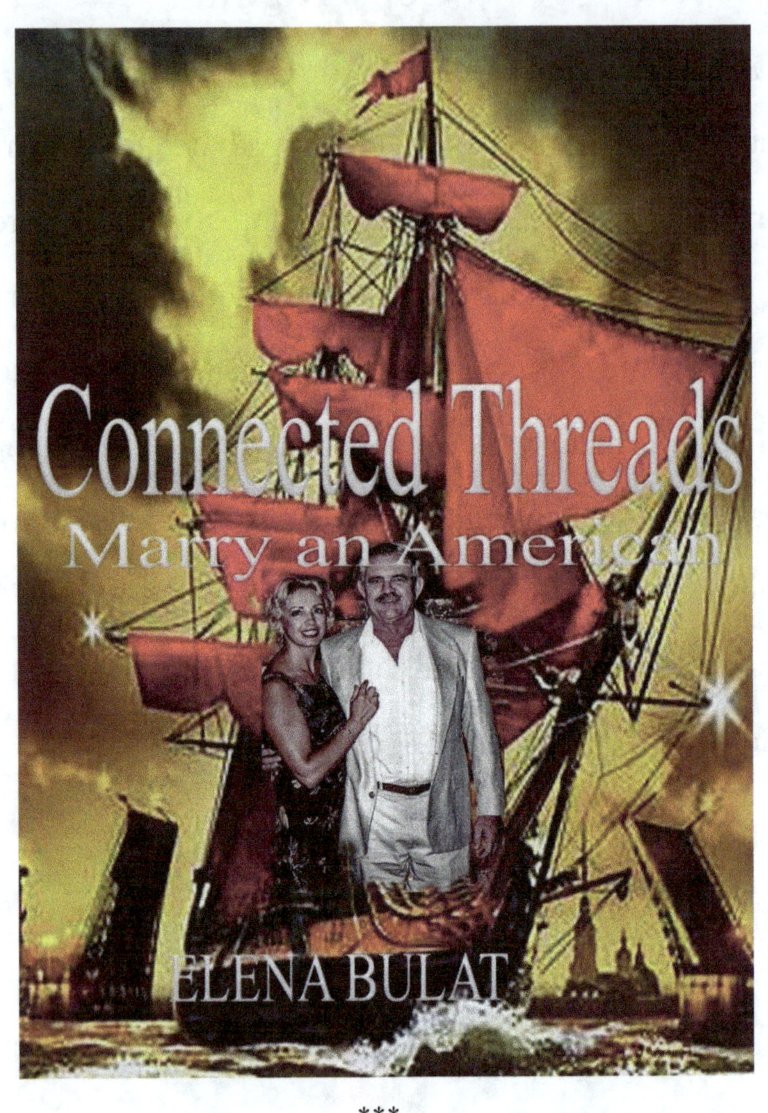

***

ISBN: 9781952907203